A Life of More

By

N. Lynn

Hasmark
PUBLISHING
INTERNATIONAL

Published by
Hasmark Publishing
www.hasmarkpublishing.com

Disclaimer

This book is designed to provide information and motivation to our readers. It is sold with the understanding that the publisher is not engaged to render any type of psychological, legal, or any other kind of professional advice. The content of each article is the sole expression and opinion of its author, and not necessarily that of the publisher. No warranties or guarantees are expressed or implied by the publisher's choice to include any of the content in this volume. Neither the publisher nor the individual author(s) shall be liable for any physical, psychological, emotional, financial, or commercial damages, including, but not limited to, special, incidental, consequential or other damages. Our views and rights are the same: You are responsible for your own choices, actions, and results.

Permission should be addressed in writing to Nancy at nancylynnofficial@gmail.com

Editor: Brad Green
brad@hasmarkpublishing.com
Cover Designer: Anne Karklins
anne@hasmarkpublishing.com
Interior layout: Amit Dey
amit@hasmarkpublishing.com

ISBN 13: 978-1-77482-004-9
ISBN 10: 1774820048

This is a work of fiction. Unless otherwise indicated, all names, characters, businesses, places, events, and incidents in this book are either the product of the author's imagination or used in a fictitious manner. Any resemblance to actual persons living or dead, or actual events is purely coincidental.

Dedicated to my Beloved.
You are the end of my rainbow.

Table of Contents

1. Prologue: More Money

"**F**ifty years!" wailed Janet. "Why has it taken me fifty years to figure this out?" If truth be told, it was all new information. She was well-read, but this particular information was something she had just heard recently for the first time. *Was it true?* She pondered. *Is every choice you make either from a place of fear or a place of love?* As she thought back on her life and the choices she made, especially in relationships, she had to admit—it sounded true. Why hadn't anyone ever told her about this? It seemed relatively simple, but then she realized that perhaps she was simply not ready to hear it until now. Well, this choice was made in love ... love for herself. Others might disagree, but she didn't care. It was her life, and that's where she found herself: with a yearning to live life on her terms without anyone else telling her what to think or how to feel. This teaching job in Dubai should fill that yearning, as it's far enough away from number three for Janet to figure out her life without the interference of any negative influences. And the money she earned from now on would be hers to spend as she liked. As Janet reflected on her life and the decisions she made, she noticed that she always seemed to be searching for something more. Little did she know, she had to be specific about the *more*.

2. More Questions

The questions continued to plague Janet:

Why am I in this place? How do I keep making the same mistakes? When will I get it right? Who am I, really? What do I want out of this life?

Deep down, she knew that her life brought her to this point because she had blatantly ignored her intuition. And every time she bailed out of difficult situations, she was a bit worse for wear.

This last time was one of them. Could she be by herself? Could she really do that? As far back as she could remember, it had never happened. She was hardly out of the last relationship, yet here she was again, starting a new one with someone she only knew through text. Tim was in the army and lived in Texas. Her online relationship with him was opening her heart to love again, and it was a distraction from the current pain. They had been texting for about six months but never spoken on the phone. Janet had planned to visit him before she left the US, but something always seemed to come up for him. Janet had experience being married to a soldier, and she knew things were never straightforward. She was very disappointed that she had to leave without ever seeing him. She had even asked her cousin Roger if she could stay with him in Fort Worth for the weekend. It was all arranged. She was ready to buy the ticket. Then Tim texted her—he had to go away for a few days. "Oh well, another time," she muttered.

It would be much harder to ever meet Tim face to face once she moved to Dubai, but she had other things to think about like this move halfway across the world. Over the years, her luck with men had been hit or miss—mostly miss—but her heart clung to the hope that she would eventually find a partner for her soul.

3. More World

Scotland – 1981

When Janet was fourteen years old, she had a religious experience of sorts—the result being a preoccupation of all things Scottish. By the end of her senior year in a parochial high school, she was obsessed. Her plan was a summer-long experience working in churches in Scotland, kindly funded by her parents. They knew not to argue with her once she made up her mind. She applied for summer mission work to a small mission board in South Carolina that had missionaries in Scotland.

With her plane ticket bought and accommodations sorted, she headed abroad.

At seventeen, she had spent her entire life in the United States. She loved her country, but something burned inside her. She wanted to leave, figuring there must be something more beyond these borders.

The first thing Janet noticed about Scotland was how green everything was. She later found out why—it rained nearly all the time. She didn't mind the rain. In fact, she quite liked it, although it often made looking her best a bit harder to accomplish. She wasn't one to normally worry about her looks, but she felt different since arriving in Scotland. She felt like something magical was going to happen, and she wanted to look her best when it did. As soon as she arrived, Janet was in love... in love with the city of Edinburgh. She loved the smell of the breweries when the wind blew in a certain direction. She loved the old buildings with their tales to tell, and the way the double-decker buses would come so close to one another she was sure they were going to crash. And of course, she loved the local accent. The second thing she noticed was how friendly everyone seemed to be, especially the young man at the church office where she would be helping for part of the summer. Sam was somewhat cute, seemed nice enough, and had a lovely accent. But there was so much to see and do that she hoped he wouldn't get in the way. In the office, he corrected her about the accent business: He wasn't the one with the accent. It was his country, and Janet was a guest. *She* had the accent. How dare she say *he* had the accent? Sam could be quite abrasive, Janet noticed. "Ok, point taken," Janet conceded. "When Americans travel abroad, *they* are the ones with the accent—not the people whose country they are visiting."

Her accommodation consisted of the entire first floor (second floor for the American reader) of an old three-story house. The church missionary couple lived on the top floor, and the office filled the ground floor. Janet was assigned odd jobs in the office. She delved into the work with fervor. Sam, the young Scottish man, felt sure that she was God's answer to his prayer for a wife. Janet wasn't so sure, as God hadn't mentioned anything to her about it. He could be quite forceful with her when she argued against this idea. Actually, he was quite forceful about everything they disagreed on. She wondered: *Were all Scottish men like this?* After spending a couple of weeks helping in the office, Janet was told she would be going to the Borders to assist a family with their summer church work where she would mostly help out with the children. She would be there for a few weeks, living with the family and their four children. Her work would consist of assisting the family with children's holiday clubs, visiting homes, and singing in the small church. Sam told her the Borders is the place where Scotland has to touch England. "Has to," he said, "because if the Scots had a choice, there would be a great chasm between the two countries." She thought the idea was a bit strange and harsh, but Sam said she would find out the hard way if she ever had the misfortune of calling a Scotsman "English."

While in the Borders, Janet enjoyed every activity and every job she was given. The family was lovely and easygoing. They would all gather around the meal table and discuss what went on that particular day. The host was very funny and kept everyone laughing. One day, the family told Janet that they were going to give her a treat—a trip up north to Loch Lomond. They would be on the road for a few hours but would pack a picnic so they could eat on the banks of the loch. Janet was excited, as her original plans had only included Edinburgh and the south. On the day of the trip they all squeezed into the little car, excited by the prospect of a picnic by the loch. As they neared the loch, Janet's host asked if she would like to drive the car. This was a risky proposition for at least three reasons. First, in the UK, drivers use the left side of the road, opposite from how she learned. In addition to that, the steering wheel was on the right! Second, the majority of cars were manual, and so was the one they were driving that day. Janet had no experience with a gear shift and clutch. And lastly, the roads around Loch Lomond were barely wide enough for one car in either direction. She took the wheel, and needless to say, it was a very stimulating drive. But her time as the driver was short-lived, as her fear of a headlong collision and burning out the clutch overwhelmed her. After a near-miss with an oncoming car, she decided it was time to be a passenger again and gladly handed the keys back over to her host.

News began to spread that Her Majesty the Queen was coming to Balmoral. Janet was excited. Her only concern was she'd have to ask for time off to go back to Edinburgh for the event. She would only be gone for the day, so her host family agreed. She would catch the bus there and back. Funny how she wasn't afraid to try new things here in this somewhat unfamiliar place. Everything was an adventure, and she could always plead ignorance as a tourist and find someone to help.

It was hot and sunny that day. Janet had been standing and walking and standing and walking, hoping to catch a glimpse of the Queen. In the end, she managed to get a few pictures, but didn't know if they'd be anything worth looking at. It was time to head back towards the Borders. The bus station was a few miles away, and she wasn't sure how to get there. Who could she ask? Just then, Janet spied two policemen who looked friendly enough. "Could you please tell me the way to the bus station?" To her surprise, they offered to give her a lift in their police car. *How exciting!* Janet thought. She sat in the back as they chatted away. "What part of America are you from? What do you do for a living? How long will you be in Scotland?" And finally, "Would you like to come to the pub for a drink?" She would still have time to catch the last bus, they assured her.

Here was Janet, a seventeen-year-old girl in a foreign country who had never tasted alcohol in her life. Up until this point, her life had been very sheltered. She attended a small church school where even the mention of alcohol was considered a sin. Should she go to the pub? They were policemen, after all. *I couldn't be any safer*, she reasoned to herself. She agreed to go for a quick drink. As they neared the pub, Janet had anxious thoughts. *Was she really in safe hands? What if she got drunk and somehow missed her bus, or worse?* "Stop!" Janet practically shouted. "Please just take me to the St. James Bus Depot." They tried to assure her everything would be fine, but she knew the best thing to do was catch the bus back to the Borders.

Love was in the air. As a big fan of Prince Charles, Janet was fortunate enough to be in the UK for the royal wedding of

Lady Diana Spencer and Prince Charles. She purchased many souvenirs to mark the occasion. She spent the day with her host family, also American, gathered around the television. What a wonderful fairy tale event this was! They celebrated as if it was their own Royal family, but she was not sure how many of their Scottish neighbors shared in their excitement. Shortly after the wedding, Janet's time in the Borders of Scotland came to an end and she headed up north, back to Edinburgh.

Sam continued to pursue Janet. He bought her fish and chips wrapped in newspaper, begged her to see the sights of the city with him, and continued to tell her that she was to be his wife. Janet was not impressed at all—that is, until the day Sam came into the office with another guy. It was Sam's best friend, Ben, who was on leave from the British Army. Having grown up in a military family, Janet was a sucker for a man in uniform. Ben wasn't wearing his uniform that day, but when she saw photos of him dressed up, she was smitten. Unlike Sam, he was quiet and mysterious, and not aggressive with his affection towards her. Ben wasn't particularly attractive, but she was drawn to him. She did everything she could to see him and be with him. She managed to take his picture, one in which Sam insisted on being in as well. She didn't care as long as Ben was in it. He lived nearby, and with not much else to do while on leave, he hung around the office quite a bit. The three would walk around the city after Sam and Janet finished their work in the office. So many feelings were flooding her heart, she thought it might burst. It was all so exciting. Her feelings for Ben were unlike anything she had ever experienced. She wondered: *is this what love feels like?*

On one of her last nights in Edinburgh, the three friends joined a tent revival service held in the Meadows (a large grassy park in Edinburgh). Knowing it would probably be her last chance to say something to Ben, she gathered up the courage, quickly scribbled her address, and slipped it to him. She leaned over and whispered in his ear, "Write to me, please!" Seeing this, Sam sensed something was happening between Ben and Janet and promptly announced it was time to leave. Janet didn't know if Ben would write, but at least she had given him the opportunity.

4. More Feelings

Arriving back in North Carolina, Janet had only a few days before she was due at a university in Georgia. She was still high from her trip to Scotland. Her three months there had been the most glorious months of her life. Before she left Scotland, she had spoken with one of the single missionary ladies and pleaded for her to intercede with the mission board so her trip could be extended. The lady said it was complicated as Janet was only on a visitor's visa, and they didn't have much work for her with the summer coming to an end. She was advised to go back to the States and start the process over from there. Janet wanted to be there now and stay forever! She was in love and knew that life in Scotland would be very exciting! Being at university was just temporary. She had no idea what she wanted to do with her life except to get married to a Scotsman.

Janet patiently waited for Ben's letters. The mailboxes at university were in another building, and she would rush over to check each day after class. She'd open the box, and when she finally saw that red, white, and blue airmail envelope, she screamed with delight. She felt so special and wanted to cry with joy and excitement. The news was good: Ben liked her and wanted to see her again! It was difficult to concentrate on her studies as she daydreamed of a life with Ben in the United Kingdom. Janet talked to Ben regularly on the dormitory phone, which was in a room at the end of the hallway. Sometimes Sam would get on the line and want to talk to Janet, but she certainly wasn't wasting her valuable time talking to him. This problem persisted so she enlisted the help of her new friend, Elise, who just so happened to be interested in working for the church in England. When Sam called wanting to talk to Janet, she would pass the phone to Elise. Janet knew that Sam was still fond of her, but there were no reciprocal feelings. As time went on, Elise and Sam began to develop a relationship. Elise was even planning a trip to England in the not-too-distant future. It would be her first time. Janet hadn't been to England, so she had no advice to offer. She was just excited because Sam wouldn't be bothering her anymore. Now she could concentrate her thoughts on Ben. Janet and Elise spent hours dreaming and planning their lives with the Scottish pair. Janet was eighteen, and in love. She finally knew what she wanted in life, and a university degree wasn't it. She was desperate to see Ben the next summer, but he was being shipped to the Falkland Islands (a British territory of tiny islands in the South Atlantic). Janet feared she wouldn't see him again and pleaded with God to make it possible for them to be together. After many months, her prayers were answered. Ben would be arriving back in England in December. Earlier that year, Ben had given Janet the contact information of a friend, in case she was ever in

England. Janet borrowed money from her brother and purchased a ticket. She flew to England to surprise Ben. The Ems, the family friends of Ben, said she could stay with them. Mr. Em would drive her to the Royal Air Force base where soldiers were returning from the Falklands. As the evening of Ben's arrival approached, Janet felt as if her heart would burst from emotion. Her love was coming back to her. Excitedly, she waited at the gate as the troops disembarked. Searching the camouflage sea of soldiers, Janet spotted Ben and flung herself into his arms. Ben was in shock as Janet was the last person he expected to see. He had lost a lot of weight and was grimy from the long hours of travel, but Janet didn't care. She was with her love once again. They headed back to town where Ben would enjoy some well-earned leave. They had a week to share together before Janet was expected back at university. At first, Janet felt strange being with Ben. After all, they had only spent a few days together the previous year in Scotland. Most of their "getting to know each other" had been done through letters and over the phone, but despite this, they seemed to get on well. The time went fast and soon it was time for Janet to leave. They promised to stay in touch, and Janet cried as she boarded the plane back to the States. She thought her heart would break into a million tiny pieces. Was this true love? Had she truly found the man she was to love for the rest of her life? How long before they could be together again?

5. More Change

The next summer, Janet changed to a university closer to her home in North Carolina. She still didn't know what she wanted to do with her life or what she wanted to study, but one thing Janet did know for certain was that she wanted to marry Ben. As the months passed, she and Ben continued to correspond and speak on the phone. Ben's phone bill was enough to buy two plane tickets (money he couldn't afford on his wages as a soldier), but they didn't care. They were recklessly in love. Janet longed more than ever to leave this country of her birth and see what the rest of the world had to offer. She finally got her wish. In August, Ben and Janet married. They had a quick honeymoon, then flew back to England. At nineteen years old, Janet was joyously optimistic at what the future held.

If we could look inside Janet's mind, perhaps we would see that she had really based her decision on where she wanted to be, not caring how she got there or who she was with. She had set out to make life decisions based on how she wanted things to be. She wanted something more than the life she had previously known. As a young teen, Janet filled her mind with stories of innocent love and romance. She believed in finding her prince and living happily ever after. Her dream was to live in the UK—Scotland to be precise—and although she found herself living in England and married to a Scotsman, it was close enough to keep her happy ... for a while.

Ben was a young private in the British Army, a Falklands War veteran, and Janet was a teenager in love. He told her he loved her. Why else would he marry her? But in actuality, what did either of them know about love? She wasn't sure she ever really saw love between her own parents. Ben's parents seemed to get on well, but more as friends than anything else. Janet was looking for a relationship filled with love. Perhaps if she wanted it bad enough, the deep, true love would come. After all, how difficult could it be to have a marriage full of love?

6. More Heedlessness

After Ben and Janet married, they moved to a small town close to Ben's work. They rented a room belonging to an elderly lady until army housing could be found, as there was a waiting list. Quite soon, sharing the house with the old lady and her dog proved problematic, so Ben found a large room in a bed and breakfast about thirty miles down the road belonging to the parents of an army buddy. Ben would ride his scooter to the army base while Janet stayed at the B&B. Ben's wages weren't great as a private, but the owners of the home were giving them a deal, meals included. It was a quiet place, and Janet filled her days by walking and visiting the local library. She also had a bike that she enjoyed riding.

The owners of the bed and breakfast seemed nice enough, until Janet and Ben had trouble coming up with the money to pay rent. Ben had to borrow money to pay the bills. As Janet and Ben were members of a church in town, Ben was fortunate enough to borrow the amount they needed from a member of the church. He went to work the next day, and on his way home he picked up the money. The owners had been holding Janet's bike as collateral until they got their rent. They didn't seem so friendly anymore and would stop talking whenever Janet entered the room. Janet was scared, as she had never been in this situation. She and Ben decided to leave. The following day, while Ben was working, a member of the church came to pick up Janet. The owners of the home were out, and Janet didn't tell them that she and Ben would be leaving; she hoped she would never see them again. She left the money they owed on the pillow of their bed. But what about her bike? It was locked in their storage room. She knew there must be a key. As luck would have it, she found it without much searching. Janet didn't make a habit of searching for keys to locked doors in other people's homes, but she felt justified in this case. She loaded her bike into the van with the rest of their belongings. They drove off, and Janet felt safe once again.

Janet and Ben were allowed to stay at another church member's house until other accommodations could be found. Months later, after several more moves, Janet and Ben ended up getting an army flat near his base. It was already furnished with typical army furniture, not very modern, but boxy and practical. Janet made it as cozy as she could. The town was a quiet army town with small local shops surrounded by army housing. Janet didn't know anyone in the new town, and the only people she did know were from the church and lived miles away. They couldn't afford a car. Having more time on her hands than she knew what to do with, she found herself growing restless, wanting some sort of job. With no university degree, her options were limited. She searched the jobs section of the local paper and saw a cleaning job. The only problem was the location, almost eleven miles away. How would she get there? The bus didn't run regularly, but Janet was young and healthy so three times a week she cycled the twenty-two miles roundtrip to the cleaning job on the outskirts of the big town. She only worked there for about two months, because Ben soon got a posting order to Germany.

It was October 1984. Once again, they would have to wait for housing. Janet did not want to wait in the army flat and be away from Ben, but what choice did she have? As luck would have it, some family friends from North Carolina had recently moved to the Netherlands. Janet's mother was in contact with them, so she gave Janet their phone number. After Janet spoke with them and explained the situation, they gladly offered her a place to stay for as long as she needed. Ben would live in army barracks in Germany while Janet would visit him by train whenever she could, as the base in Germany was only an hour and a half from her friend's home in the Netherlands. Janet lived there for three months. In January of 1985, Ben and Janet were given a little flat in a small German town near the army base. It was a lovely two-bedroom flat right above a bakery. Janet would get up early and get fresh brotchen (bread rolls) or whatever she fancied. Once again, she found herself with more time than she wanted and no job. Because Janet wasn't fluent in German, her options were limited to the local NAAFI (Navy, Army, Air Force Institutes). It was a shop that stocked British products for the families stationed overseas. She would go there most days. As luck would have it, she saw a cleaning job and applied, but she was not overly hopeful as there were more women than jobs available. The manager seemed to like it that Janet was a Yank, as there were not many Americans married to British soldiers, so he gave her the job. A few weeks after Janet started, she found out that she was pregnant. She couldn't believe it. This was what she had been waiting for: a baby to raise in a loving home. She and Ben still didn't have a lot of money, so Janet bought most things second hand from the other wives, and worked right up until a month before she was due, in October.

Between the two of them, Janet was the only driver. She enlisted the help of a pastor friend who would drive her to the hospital when the time came. Almost exactly on her due date, Janet's water broke. Ben called the pastor who sped over to pick them up. It was a cold, wet October day when their son Tony made his entrance by an emergency Caesarian section. Janet was put into a single room to recover, as it was a major operation. She stayed in hospital for seven days, and with every day she fell more in love with their child. "Oh, the hopes and dreams we hold for our children when they arrive in our care," mused Janet. She knew she was going to love being a mother.

Tony was a delightful baby and Janet felt blessed to be able to stay home and care for him. But in the spring of 1986, when Tony was about six months old, the Chernobyl nuclear disaster occurred. The fallout was far-reaching, and Janet's mother pleaded with her to come back to the States, at least for a little while, to give her young baby a healthy environment. Ben and Janet had visited the States once when Tony was four months old. He was the first grandchild on her family's side, so Janet's mother had been eagerly awaiting him. But it was during that trip that Ben told Janet that he had slept with their neighbor while she was in hospital with Tony. He was truly sorry. The shock of this news made Janet wonder if she had made the right choice for a husband. Wasn't she good enough? Wasn't she pretty or sexy enough for him? It was a strong blow to her already fragile self-esteem. Devastated by his confession, Janet still held to the belief that it was wrong to end a marriage. She decided to try to get past Ben's infidelity and keep their young family together.

On their return to Germany early that September, Ben had news that an army quarter was ready for them. They moved the short distance to the new place, but unbeknownst to Janet at the time, she had become pregnant again; she found out when she began to bleed heavily. Whether it was the stress of the move or that her body simply wasn't ready for another baby, Janet had a miscarriage. She believed it was because she wasn't ready, but shortly after, as life would have it, she became pregnant for a third time. Janet was sent to the doctor to see if she would be able to deliver this baby naturally. After an x-ray, it was clear she would have to deliver this baby, and any future babies, by C-section. Her pelvis was wrongly shaped and no baby of hers would survive a normal delivery. On the plus side, she would know exactly when the baby was coming, as she was given a date for the operation. Eva was delivered on a lovely April morning. Ben was still in the process of getting his driving license, so he wasn't able to drive her to the hospital. His boss, Bill Cotter, whose wife Lindsay had become good friends with Janet, would drive them. The Cotters didn't have any children of their own, so they made themselves available to drive Ben and Tony whenever they wanted to visit Janet and Eva.

7. More History

Having two young children nineteen months apart was a real challenge. Janet remembered something she once heard: "People with only one child are not real parents." For her, it was spot on. As she juggled marriage and motherhood with everyday life, her discontent began to grow. She needed to get out of the house, to feel like she was more than just a mother. So, in April 1989, Janet planned a trip. The whole family would take the British troop train to West Berlin. At that time, Berlin was located deep inside communist East Germany, but the troop train had access straight from West Germany to the western part of Berlin. While in West Berlin, Janet and Ben wanted to travel to East Berlin and stock up on cheap electrical equipment and cameras. Many things were involved in planning this trip because Janet was an American citizen and had to be granted permission from the U.S. Embassy. Ben, being a British citizen, would have to get the necessary paperwork for himself and the two children, who had dual citizenship, and would use their British passports for the trip. The trip was planned for November seventh through tenth, 1989.

Janet's little family arrived in Berlin on the evening of November seventh. After settling into their army hostel accommodation, they rested as the next day would be busy. Janet was looking forward to visiting Checkpoint Charlie—the gateway to eastern Berlin. On the evening of the eighth of November, the family caught the underground train to the main part of the city. It was bustling with people. There were long lines of people outside the banks. *Weren't they closed this time of night?* thought Janet. They tried to catch the train back to the hostel, but each train was jam-packed. They had to wait for at least three trains before they could squeeze in. Arriving back at their accommodation, Janet put on the television to see if she could find out what was happening. To her disbelief, communism in East Berlin (East Germany) had begun to crumble and the Berlin Wall was about to come down. The next day they traveled to the heart of the city to the location of the Wall. People shouted at the guards who were standing on top of the wall near the Brandenburg Gate, while others were chipping away at it. As they walked around the city, all they could see were Travees, standard East German cars, filling every space. It seemed the city's population had tripled overnight. Janet and Ben asked a passerby why the people were lining up at the banks. The man told them that every East Berliner would receive DM100 (Deutsch Marks) as a gift from the West German government to welcome them back. Germany would be united once again.

Janet and Ben never did get to Checkpoint Charlie or buy any cheap electrical goods from the East, but what they did get was far greater—they witnessed a part of history.

8. More of Love's Sweet Dream

Life went on, but Janet once again became restless. She wanted more: more love, more excitement, more purpose. She was living a mundane life, and she hated it. She didn't hate her children; she loved being able to stay home with them. But she hated that nothing new ever happened in her life. Things were growing stale between her and Ben. She didn't know how to change even if she wanted to. When Janet married Ben, she vowed to never divorce and that she would give any children they had a happy home. As time went on, she realized she'd probably never be happy in this marriage, but she also recognized that this was a heavy price to pay. Still, she resigned herself to her fate. Little did she know what love and happiness lay around the corner.

It came in the form of a man named Kyle, a soldier who worked with Ben. Whenever Ben spoke of Kyle, Janet felt like she knew him. It was a bizarre feeling because she had never met him. One day, Ben invited Kyle over for dinner. He had wrecked his motorcycle and was in need of some TLC. The very moment he walked into her home Janet felt a spark of recognition. He was tall, handsome, and easygoing. They had a great time that evening. She, Ben and Kyle played board games, took the kids for a walk, and enjoyed a lovely meal. Later, Ben had to take Kyle back. About fifteen minutes after they left, the phone rang. It was Kyle. He wanted to thank her for a lovely time. Then he said, "If I were your husband, I would never let you out of my sight. I'd want to spend all my time with you." Janet marvelled, "Oh my God." He had read her mind. Over the next few weeks, Kyle came to their home frequently. When they played games, Kyle and Janet found an uncontrollable urge to sit next to each other and touch their legs under the table. Kyle's touch was like electricity being shot through her body. It wasn't quite a sexual feeling, but more the feeling of being connected to a part of herself that she never knew. Janet and Kyle managed to steal small snippets of moments together. She always made excuses why Kyle should be invited over. When they were apart, they could sense each other's thoughts. One day, while Ben was on duty, he had arranged with Kyle to take Janet on the back of his newly restored motorcycle. She had never been on a motorcycle before and was ecstatic to share the experience with Kyle. The kids would stay with Ben for an hour or so while she and Kyle went for the ride. Janet was not aware that Ben knew of her feelings towards Kyle, but she figured if he had felt threatened, he would not have arranged this ride. They rode on the autobahn, speeding up to 130 kilometers an hour. Janet thought she would fly right off the back of the bike but held on tightly to Kyle. It felt so good to hold him, so natural. They took full advantage of their time alone and stopped off for ice cream in town. Although neither of them could speak much German, the waiter delivered their ice cream with a heart clip that said "I love you" in English. Could the worker feel the love that Janet and Kyle felt for each other? Every spare moment that Janet wasn't thinking about her children, she was thinking about Kyle. There had not been anything physical between them, but not for want of trying on Janet's part. She tried to plan other rendezvous so they could be alone, but the opportunities never materialized.

Each moment Kyle and Janet spent together caused their feelings to grow stronger. Janet would do anything to be with Kyle. Ben was due to go on a week-long exercise while Kyle was house-sitting for a friend. Janet arranged to spend a couple of nights at the house with Kyle and the children. The first day was unbelievably happy for Janet, and she could sense it in Kyle too. They had a barbecue, ate ice cream, and played with the kids in the back yard. It was as if they were truly a family. Janet was not sure how Ben found out, but early one morning they were awoken by a banging on the door. It was Ben, and he was angry. He demanded that she and the children leave with him at once. Begrudgingly, she went with him but was embarrassed that he had found out about Kyle and her in that way.

Janet knew she didn't love Ben and wanted to take the children and be with Kyle. She even talked to Kyle about her plans, but he told her in no uncertain terms that although he loved her, he would never be the reason for the break up of a marriage. If he only knew how broken she and Ben were already.

A few weeks later, Kyle took a trip to Canada. Janet had a feeling that he would meet someone there. When Kyle returned, he showed her a picture of a girl. She had blonde hair like Janet's. How was she ever going to let the love of her life go? The feelings she had for Kyle were celestial and tangible at the same time. They were unlike any she felt for Ben, even at the beginning. Kyle was the man she should have married. He was the man she wanted to marry. How could she come so close to her soul mate, and then be forced to let him go and settle for a banal existence?

Ben and Janet tried to get past what had happened with her and Kyle. He even surprised Janet with a visit from Kyle before he left for the UK. He was being discharged from the army and would spend his last night in their flat. Janet got up in the middle of the night pretending to go to the bathroom but headed towards his room instead. As she stood outside his door, it took every ounce of strength in her body not to open the door and go inside to be with him one last time. The next morning when Ben was busy with the children, Janet whispered in Kyle's ear, "I'll never forget you. I hope we meet again someday." However, they both knew the chances of that were slim.

9. More Children

In late 1991, having moved to another base in Germany, Janet became pregnant again. She had friends and acquaintances ask, why would she have another child when her older two were in school and she finally had time to herself? Janet never told anyone the reason, but it was from a chance remark made by a friend when she, Ben, and the two children were having dinner at the friend's house. This couple had two grown children, and the wife said she always regretted not having more. Why this remark stuck in Janet's head, she'll never know. Ben and Janet's third child Ella was born on a cold March day in 1992. She was a colicky baby, who slept very little. Janet was left feeling exhausted and found it difficult to care properly for the other two children. Eva was happy to have a baby sister and loved spending time with her. As she grew, Ella proved to be a delightful addition to the family. Ben didn't seem to be around much, but that was fine with Janet. They didn't have much to talk about except for the children.

While still in Germany, Ben was sent to Bosnia. He had only been gone for a few months when Janet found out she was pregnant again. She was on her own with three small children and one on the way. Ben asked an ex-soldier friend,

Daniel, who lived in Germany, to come and look after Janet while he was away. Janet could call Daniel if she had an emergency and it helped that he spoke German. Daniel was fun to have around. He made her laugh. He would play with the kids, giving Janet short breaks. He even took her and the children out for picnics in the woods. Actually, Janet was happier to have Daniel around than she was with Ben, as she and Daniel never argued and they both just enjoyed spending time together, and with the kids. Janet once again found herself wanting another man—someone other than her husband. Why did she seem to fall in love so easily? Were these men really any different from Ben?

As the time to deliver baby number four grew closer, Ben called and said the army wouldn't release him from his time in Bosnia to come home for the birth. Janet was fuming! How was she supposed to cope? She was having a major operation and had three children under eight years old. Ben suggested she get the doctor or a health visitor to write or call and request that he was needed and should be sent back. In the end, Ben did come back, but having this fourth child made more cracks in the foundation of an already shaky marriage.

In January 1994, Ben received orders back to England. They had been in Germany for nine years, and baby Cameron was only eight weeks old. They had two cars, so it would be a feat to get them back to the UK. Ben would handle that part. Janet would go by plane with the four children and arrive at the RAF base where Ben would be waiting to pick them up.

Fortunately, this time they had army housing ready and waiting for them. Janet found the house relatively smaller than the flat in Germany. She was very frustrated with the layout, but at least it had some kind of garden. The move had been difficult. Unpacking and setting up the house, all the while caring for four children: a baby only a few weeks old, a twenty-month-old toddler, a seven-year-old, and an eight-year-old. Money was short, too. Ben's wages had been cut as they were not entitled to the extra money they received while living in Germany. With bills piling up and Janet suffering postpartum depression, their marriage began to rapidly deteriorate. Ben was spending more time away. He would not say where he was going, but Janet did not care. She had too many things to worry about. She even tried to earn some extra money looking after a set of twins who lived next door. But how was she supposed to do that with her own four children needing to be cared for? Didn't she have enough to do already? Most of the time Janet felt like she was being slowly suffocated. She had to get out, to go somewhere—anywhere. During these moments, Janet was extremely thankful she had a car and could leave the house, the mayhem, and that stifling feeling. The few times in her life when Janet didn't have a car, she felt like someone had cut her legs off. In truth, Janet was exhausted all the time, frustrated with the lack of money for even the essentials, rushing to get the children into the local school, signing up with the medical centre, and generally trying to settle back into life in England. In spite of all this busyness, Janet felt unsettled, still wanting something more.

10. More Lies

After some time, Janet came to realize what Ben had been doing in his time away from home. He had been spending time with a fifteen-year-old girl, taking her out in his Land Rover, sometimes taking their two older kids along as well. At first, Janet thought nothing of it. Why should she? Ben said he was just helping her with some climbing skills, and they would be with a group of people. Anyway, Ben was Janet's husband—she bore his children for God's sake! And most of all, she still felt very attractive. Janet wouldn't consider that young girl any kind of a threat. But as time went on, she started to get a sick feeling in her stomach. One morning, she went out to Ben's Land Rover and looked around. There was an earring on the floor by his seat, and it was not Janet's. He had just returned from taking their two older children swimming. She returned to the house and asked the two children if anyone else had gone swimming with them besides their dad. Tony became quiet, but Eva said Dad drove to a house and picked up a girl. Janet challenged Ben about his motives for spending time with this girl, but he continued to argue that they were just friends.

Shortly after, Ben decided to move out. He said he needed space to think about things, so he moved into the Sergeant's mess. Janet did not have any real proof of an affair, but by God, her gut kept telling her something was going on between the two. Whenever she confronted Ben, he strongly denied everything. One day Janet needed to talk to Ben, so she drove over to the mess to find him. The desk sergeant said he wasn't there, so she asked where his room was. He told her it was around the back part of the building on the ground floor. Janet left the sergeant but stealthily went around the building and found the window to Ben's room. Fortunately, it was open. Janet didn't make a habit of climbing into windows, and if she were caught, who knows what would have happened. She knew she didn't have much time to look before someone saw her, so she acted quickly. There on the bedside table was a pair of sexy black underwear. Swiftly, Janet climbed back out the window, the underwear in her pocket. Later, she confronted Ben with the underwear, and once again, he said he and the fifteen-year-old were only friends. Janet's stomach tightened. She knew he was lying this time. Why, then, did she still want to believe him? She was still young and in the prime of her life. Some men would be proud to be seen with her. Why would he risk his marriage and family to be with a fifteen-year-old? Janet spent most of her days crying and trying to look after the four children. She knew she needed help, so she went to a doctor. He prescribed her what would be her first batch of antidepressant medicine. He said it would help her cope with things. Little did Janet know she would continue taking the medication on and off for the next twenty-plus years.

One evening, Ben was supposed to be on duty and Janet needed to see him about childcare arrangements. The guards told her that he wasn't there. There was only one other place he could be, and Janet had a rough idea where it was. She drove into town and found the teenage girl's house, and there out front was an army Land Rover. Janet knocked on the door. The girl's mother answered. Janet calmly stated, "I need to speak to my husband." The woman sneered, "Well, he doesn't want to speak to you!" She slammed the door in Janet's face. What had Ben been telling them about her? What was she to do? Janet felt humiliated but couldn't just walk away. Then she remembered there was a can of gold spray paint in her car. She took the paint and sprayed some choice words on the army Land Rover. At this point, she didn't care if Ben got into trouble. She was in extreme pain. Tears flowed down Janet's face. What would happen next?

Later, when she saw Ben, she confronted him about this girl. He was still vexed about the Land Rover incident. She had caused him a lot of trouble. It was army property. Janet screamed, "What about us? What about our marriage and children?" Ben answered that he was confused but still maintained that he and the girl were just friends. Janet couldn't believe what she was hearing. She ranted, "I won't play second fiddle to anyone! If you don't want to be with me then

I will file for divorce." She couldn't live like this. She didn't want to live like this!

It was nearing the school summer holiday, and Janet decided to take the four children to visit her parents in the States, as they loved spending time with their grandchildren. They could fly standby on a VC10 for a very small amount of money. The RAF base was not far away, and she could leave the car parked there while they were away. As Janet prepared to leave for the trip, a voice told her to look in Ben's car. She "borrowed" the keys and in the back, under a cushion, she found a camera. She took it and packed it with her things.

The morning they set out for their trip to the States, Janet tried to be cheerful. She had a feeling that the film in the camera would quell any doubt about whether Ben was having an affair. She loaded the kids into the seven-seat Peugeot. While driving, she didn't know why she chose to overtake another car where and when she did. With a car oncoming she slowed down and tried to get back over into the correct lane, but it was too late.

Janet and the children were taken to the nearest hospital. By the grace of God, no one was hurt. It had been a head-on collision, and Janet would most likely be charged. She begged the policeman to let them go, as they had a flight to catch. They let her go, telling her they'd be in touch. The hospital staff told her they would call a taxi. Where did she want to go? Janet told them to take her and the children to the RAF base. She desperately wanted to catch that flight, but by the time they arrived, their plane had already left. She asked the clerk when they could try for another flight. He said to come back in two days and then asked Janet if she wanted to call someone to come and get them. Janet gave him Ben's work number, and he handed her the phone. Ben was busy and couldn't get off duty, or so he claimed. He would call his civilian friend, Ivan, to come pick them up. Truthfully, Janet felt guilty endangering her children with this accident, but when Ben said he couldn't get off duty to pick them up, she knew their marriage was finished. He didn't care whether they lived or died.

Two days later Janet and the children arrived in the United States. It was a fun, relaxing time as Janet's parents spoiled them with days out, dinners in restaurants, and Janet, with some time to herself. They spent most days at the condominium pool trying to keep cool from the summer heat. With time to think, Janet was bothered about the condition of her marriage. Could she really end it and be a single parent to these four beautiful children? How could she divorce, as it was against her beliefs? She had been taught that divorce was wrong. The truth was that Janet's heart was brimming with pain. She believed she had been betrayed by Ben once again, and she just wanted the pain to go away. Indifferent to the repercussions of the action she would take, she just wanted relief from this pain, whatever it took.

Janet got the film developed. She looked at the photos in disbelief, but her first thought was, *who took the pictures?* Then the realization of what it meant dawned on her and her suspicions were confirmed. There was Ben and the girl in bed together. She didn't want to believe it, but there it was staring her in the face—it was the proof she didn't want to acknowledge. Janet thought that knowing the truth would release some of her pain, but how wrong she was. Her pain was only intensified. Once again, Janet had time to think about her marriage and she wasn't happy with the thoughts. Her feelings emerged into a cocktail of betrayal, uselessness, loneliness, humiliation, hopelessness—but the worst of all was the feeling of being unloved and unwanted. The pain she felt was not like anything she had ever experienced. It was unbearable. When she and the children returned to England, she would have to figure out what to do next.

Janet continued to take her medication hoping it would keep the tears away. She didn't want the kids to see her crying all the time. As the time approached for them to leave the States, part of Janet was relieved because she wanted to be back in her own place. She loved her parents, but her mother could often be harsh about Janet's parenting skills. But what would happen when they got back? What would Janet do about this sham of a marriage?

When they arrived back at the house, Ben greeted them with some news. He was being sent on a short tour of duty to Northern Ireland. Janet felt some relief. She didn't want to be around him at the moment, but she knew she wanted to challenge him with the pictures found on the film in his camera. Once the children had settled into bed, Janet declared that she wanted a divorce. Ben lied to her again and again. He could have that girl, as far as Janet was concerned. She had enough of his lies. Ben fell silent. With time away from Janet and the kids, he had been thinking too. He didn't want a divorce. He would end things with the girl. They could both take some more time and decide what they wanted while he was in Northern Ireland. Janet didn't answer him. *Maybe,* she thought to herself. *Maybe they should try again, for the sake of the children.* For whatever reason, Ben's tour of Northern Ireland was cut short and a couple of things happened when he returned. First, while Janet was cleaning up Ben's things, she found several letters amongst his belongings. They were from that girl, declaring her love for him and saying she was anxious to be with him when he returned. The other was far more serious than the previous, for a different reason. While Janet was home one day, the military police came to the door and demanded that she let them search the house. She inquired about what they were looking for. They told her they were looking for weapons. "Weapons?" questioned Janet, anxiously. "What kind of weapons? How did they get here? Why would there be weapons in the house with children around?" The officers insisted they needed to have a look around. As they searched, Janet continued to explain that she was unaware of any weapons in the house. She had four young children to look after. As they continued their search, Janet fretted, "What the hell is going on?"

The older of the two officers said that Ben was being investigated. He had access to weapons, and they had been tipped off about some suspicious activity. On searching Janet's bedroom, they found a replica of an army rifle behind some ceiling tiles. Stunned with disbelief and tears in her eyes, Janet asked what would happen next. The men told her that Ben would probably be charged first, then sentenced. They wouldn't know any more until the investigation was finished. Janet's head was reeling. *Oh my God! What was happening? First the girl, now this!*

Ben was still living in the Sergeant's mess and Janet didn't know if he had any idea what was happening at home. A few days later, Ben came to the house. He had taken some pills. Janet saw the state he was in, but she was sick of the mess that he had made for himself. She didn't want to have anything to do with him. Janet told him that he couldn't stay, no matter what happened. It was all too much, and she didn't want the children to see their father as he tried to self-destruct. Fortunately, Janet's friend, who was visiting at the time, had some first aid training, and seeing the severity of Ben's condition, called for an ambulance. Janet didn't think about the incident again until a few weeks later when there was another knock on the door. A policeman said Ben had been in a motorcycle accident, but no one else was involved. They thought the accident was deliberate. When he was released from hospital, Ben came to stay with Janet. She was sick and tired of Ben and his antics. Her concern now was the safety and welfare of her four young children and in this moment, she really didn't care what happened to him. Little did she know this was not the end of things. A few days later, the civil police came to her home to inform her that Ben had been arrested. "What has he done now?" Janet was seething. All the officer could tell her was that Ben had been pulled over for speeding. When the policeman approached the car, Ben told the cop that he had a gun, and that the policeman should take it from him before he used it on one of them. The officer managed to talk Ben into giving him the weapon. He was now in a local prison, awaiting sentencing. (Note to the American reader: British police are not issued guns as a rule.)

The incident made the local paper, but fortunately didn't mention any names. Janet and her children were still living in army housing, and local gossip could be unnerving. Thoughts of her children consumed her. Fortunately, the younger two had no idea what was happening to their father, but what about the older two? How would this affect them? Janet didn't have answers to their questions and tried to distract the children with trips to the park and the promise of ice cream.

With Ben in prison, Janet decided she and the children should visit him. For whatever reason, she believed the children needed to see their father. She had never ventured near a prison in her life, much less visited someone she knew. It was all surreal, like something from a movie. The visits were short, but after a few times, Janet figured perhaps it was better for the children not to see their father in such a place.

Three months later Ben was transferred to an army psychiatric hospital to be treated for post-traumatic stress disorder (PTSD). The police would not be pressing charges. Eventually, Janet found out that when Ben was serving in Bosnia, he had seen many young children dead on the side of the road—casualties of the fighting. Memories of these children were given as the cause of his PTSD and his unpredictable behavior. Janet couldn't imagine living with those images, and truly hoped Ben would get the help he needed. Bearing all this in mind, Janet reasoned that she still couldn't remain married to him. She had to take the children and start a new life away from all of this.

While Ben was in the psychiatric hospital, she filed for divorce. She didn't have any money of her own to speak of and could not afford to hire a lawyer. She got the paperwork from the courthouse, filled in what she could, got Ben to sign the documents, and returned them with the fee. She would have to wait a few weeks for her divorce plea to be heard in court. The letter came quicker than she imagined. The divorce would be granted in six weeks. Surprisingly, it was relatively easy to end an eleven-year marriage.

11. More Heartache

Janet was still living with her four children in the army quarters. With circumstances being what they were, she would have to move out as she was no longer an army wife. She was sad to leave the house as she had grown used to its convoluted design, but she had no choice. They were being relocated to a three-bedroom bungalow in a small village about thirty miles away.

Janet was thankful for the welfare system in the UK. During this trying and difficult time, they had arranged the new housing for her and her four children. The army provided a truck to move their things.

At first glance, Janet liked the village. Things were within walking distance to the school, the post office, a corner shop, and a library. The neighbor on her left side, another ex-army wife, seemed friendly. She told Janet if she ever needed anything just to come and ask.

The bungalow was small but had a garden with woods behind it. She got the children some ferrets as pets, and a couple of cats. Truth be told, it was the children who got the cats. There always seemed to be someone giving away kittens. She and the children were suckers for those tiny balls of fluff. Life kept Janet busy, taking care of the children and trying to make ends meet. She was fortunate to still own a car, unreliable as it was. It worked often enough to carry them away from the village, to another town, or just to a playpark. But there never seemed to be enough money.

Janet didn't know what she expected as a single mother, but it was nothing like this new reality. Being on welfare was an enigma. Having grown up in a middle-class American home, money always seemed to be available. But not now. How many times had the electricity been turned off because there was no money left on the electricity key? (A small key which needed to be recharged with money paid at the local shop. The key controlled the use of electricity for the bungalow.) How many times had they run out of coal for the fire, which was used to heat the house and water? Fortunately, Janet had made a friend when she joined a singing group a couple of years prior and had kept in contact with her. Amy knew of Janet's hardships, and out of the goodness of her heart periodically had coal delivered to their bungalow. It was incredible that Amy always seemed to know when Janet was running out of coal. Janet considered Amy her very own guardian angel.

Janet was glad to get out of the marriage with Ben, but her self-esteem had taken a big hit. Even being in a new place, away from all the craziness from her prior situation, she couldn't get it out of her head that she, at thirty years old, had been replaced by a teenager. Now she was in her early thirties and still very attractive, but would any man ever want her again?

She felt worthless as a woman. She was unemployed, with no university education, four children, no husband, and living on very little income. She wanted to provide for her children, to give them a life like the one she had growing up, but she felt that she couldn't do it alone. Janet perused the ads in the lonely hearts section of the local newspaper. Surely there was some man that wanted to be with an attractive woman and her four children. After weeks of searching, she found what she was looking for: "Romantic, kind-hearted gentleman, late thirties, divorced, well-read, loves classical music, looking for a soul mate." She gathered up the courage to call the number. They would meet in a nearby town, somewhere neutral.

When Janet first met Jay, she was pleasantly surprised. He was tall, had a gentle demeanor, and did indeed seem very kind. She had the four children with her to judge his reaction, but children weren't an issue as he had three of his own living with his ex-wife in a town nearby. Although Jay was unemployed and didn't have a driver's license, he came across as very intelligent. He wanted to study landscaping at a local horticultural college. With his ideas and training, he one day hoped to start a business. Janet didn't see his current unemployment as anything to worry about. Janet and Jay met up frequently in the weeks that followed. She was in love once again. No scrap heap for her. Jay had a way with words and she no longer felt ugly and unwanted. To him, she was beautiful. What did it matter that they had only known each other a few months? She was smitten. Jay moved into her small bungalow. When February fourteenth came around, being a leap year, she proposed to him. They married in a registry office and had a small reception at a friend's house.

In a matter of weeks, Janet found herself asking some serious questions: *Is it true that love is blind? Or is it only blind until you get married? If you are not honest with yourself about life, do unwanted things happen?* Jay's warm words had turned ice cold. He had a way of talking to her and the children as if they were always wrong. *Only stupid people thought or said things like that. Didn't they know his way was the correct way?* Emotional pain had become her new normal. Why, oh why, had she rushed into this marriage? She had no idea it would turn out this way. Maybe she was not the marrying kind. Deep down Janet knew she wanted to prove to herself that she was still attractive and could get a man to love her, even marry her. But now, too late, Janet realized she had paid a high price for the affection she was looking for. She was back on the anti-depressants.

Three months later, Janet's oldest son Tony couldn't stand Jay's words any longer and asked his dad if he could live with him. Janet loved her children and wanted them with her, but Tony said he couldn't live with Jay. Eva was heartbroken when Tony left, as the two of them had always been close. She was next to go. Ben broke the news to Janet. Devastation ran through Janet's body, as her children were everything to her. She was fortunate to be in a country where she didn't have to go out to work. She could stay home and take care of her children, but never in her wildest dreams did she envision any of them living apart from her. How did this happen? Why did she let it happen? Trapped in a marriage that had driven two of her children away, Janet knew she had to do something.

Janet didn't have much experience being in a verbally abusive relationship. Husband number one didn't really say much at all, and only when he was angry did she know what he was really thinking. Janet was strong-willed and stubborn by nature, but hearing someone who's supposed to love her tell her over and over again, "You are useless! I can see that you're not very smart," or "Other women would be glad to be married to a man like me. You don't know how good you have it!" all fed into her insecurities. Those words slowly replaced her truth of who she was. She slowly began to give her power over to Jay and his words, and she started to believe them. As Janet fought for her emotional survival, the realization dawned on her again—she had to get out of this marriage. She had to rescue her children, her sanity, and her fragile self-esteem.

There was a big problem. When Janet married Jay, he swore that he would never be homeless again. His first wife had done that to him, and he wasn't ever going to let that happen again. He was going nowhere. If she wanted to leave, then she could. Janet knew she had to somehow make him be the one to go.

She had an idea. She would start giving Jay's words back to him. It was worth a try. Every time he said she was useless and wanted a woman who would appreciate him, Janet said that was a great idea. *Why should he waste his life with her—someone who didn't know how intelligent and wonderful he was?* "Go for it! Find your ideal woman," she declared.

Over time, Jay agreed that they should divorce but he would not be leaving the family home. Janet implemented the next part of her plan. Since Jay was now busy with work, she would find him a place to live. Janet dedicated her free time to this; the sooner he left, the sooner she would be free. It wasn't easy to find a place that met with Jay's criteria, and his budget was limited. Janet pressed on and eventually found a place that would work for him. She and Jay went to see it together. It had plenty of room for his landscaping materials. As fate would have it, Jay loved the place. Now he could pursue whomever he wanted.

Janet had to make sure the move happened, so she began moving his things. She made as many trips as necessary to clear his stuff from the house. When it was complete, Janet was ecstatic but tried not to show it. She reminded Jay how happy he would be now that he could find the girl of his dreams. As of late, his ideal girl seemed to be Russian, but Janet didn't care if she was from Mars as long as Jay was away from her and her children.

With Jay gone, Janet tried to get Tony and Eva to move back with her and the younger two children, but sadly, they had settled in with their dad and his new wife. Janet did see them most weekends as she was only a couple of hours away, but she still missed them terribly.

12. More Friends

Throughout Janet's entire life, she had been blessed with good, caring friends. Friends who were there for her. Friends who supported her, especially in her time of crisis. One of her closest friends was Marta. She was an older widow, but they got on famously. If Janet needed the odd babysitter, Marta was always available. She lived nearby, and they would often meet up to go shopping or to do their favorite thing—having a fancy coffee with cake in a specialty shop. Marta was her lifesaver during her marriage with husband number two. When Jay left Janet crying from his abusive words, Marta showed her some much-needed love and kindness. Her words were like a cool, healing balm on a raw burn. Janet remembered one time when she was to perform the lead role in a musical. On the day of the performance, once again, Jay's words had left Janet in tears. She couldn't stop crying and didn't want her face to be puffy and red for the performance later that day. She called Marta. "No, I'm not busy. Please come over," insisted Marta. When Janet arrived, Marta was sitting out in the garden. With gentleness, she assured Janet that Jay's words were wrong. He only said those things to make himself feel better. The truth of what Marta was saying began to sink in, and thanks to her, Janet was able to perform her part that night in the musical with clear eyes and a feeling of power. She recognized that Marta had come into her life for a reason.

13. More Plans

After Jay, Janet wasn't in a hurry to marry again. She needed time to herself ... time to figure out what she really wanted in life. Deep down, she knew she had to go back to university. Janet believed that without a degree she could never get a good-paying job. She wanted to be able to care for her children and be financially independent. One day, Janet saw an advertisement for Open University. As a single mother, the course would be free. That was it! She would start with that. The course material would come by post, she would complete it, then return the work back by post to be marked by the tutor. Janet was still unsure of what her interests were, so she started with a course in humanities. She had three months to finish the entire course, and there would also be a special weeklong summer session held at Bath University. In between taking care of the children and the house, Janet completed her coursework. She felt that she did her best. This was just the beginning, and she would continue until she received a degree. She waited anxiously for her final marks to come. She opened the letter and couldn't believe what it read: *Failed.*

Janet thought her time feeling stupid and useless was a thing of the past. But once again, she found herself thinking about her life. Nevertheless, life has a funny way of carrying on, whether you are ready or not. She had failed the Open University course. What other options did she have? Her discontent grew. There must be something more she could do with her life than take the odd cleaning job or work in a supermarket. Her two young children were now in school and more independent. Janet had plenty of free time during the day. There must be something else she was supposed to do with her life.

She had tried to work part-time earning minimum wage, but as a result, she lost her housing benefits because the government determined that she earned "too much" to qualify for assistance. By the time she paid for childcare, she was worse off financially. It made more financial sense to not work at all.

Janet had lived with the British for almost half of her life. She loved living in England and never wanted to leave. She considered it her true home. Janet told people that her body may have been American, but her heart was British. But at this point in her life, she didn't know what to do. What did the future hold for her and her children? She couldn't see a way forward. Then one day, the answers came. The message was almost audible:

Go back to the States, Janet.

What? I don't want to. I am happy here! Well, kind of happy. What's in the States that I can't have here?

Your mother and father, and they are getting older.

But what am I supposed to do?

Go back to a community college and figure out what you want from your life.

But I tried the Open University course and failed!

Your mother always said that you could stay with her and your dad. They would help you get on your feet. Maybe with their support, you would find success.

I don't know. It's a big step. What about my other children here? I can't just leave them.

Don't worry. They will come later.

When Janet shared this news with her friends, she sounded crazy.

14. More Education

It all came together. Janet was amazed. It was as if someone had set the wheels in motion and orchestrated it all. She finally realized that being back in the States was where she was supposed to be, at least for now. She and the younger two children had settled in, but she missed her older two children and her life in England. Her desire was to go back one day, if only for a visit.

Janet wasted no time enrolling in the local community college. When she finished her two years there, she could apply to a four-year university and finish her degree—whatever degree that would be. Janet managed to find a job in a local post office that would help supplement her income. She had to take out student loans, as there was no way she could go to university and work full time to pay for her tuition and other fees. It wasn't long before the older two children joined Janet at her parents' house on the lake. Summer had begun.

It was still difficult being a single parent again, but Janet's parents lived upstairs and offered their support. Despite the busyness of her life, loneliness started to plague Janet. She had her children and between them, school, and her part-time job, things were hectic. Still, Janet longed for a loving relationship. Maybe she needed to date an American. Maybe that's where she had gone wrong.

It was her first time using the internet for dating, and she found herself on a dating site for lovers of classical music. The matches she picked could first message her, and later they could email. Janet was excited at the prospect and found pleasure in reading the many different profiles. Eventually, she found one that sounded perfect. Scot had never been married and had no children. Janet liked that because there would be nobody else's children to complicate things. He was a musician and teacher. The only issue was that he lived five hundred miles away. Janet hated the thought of a long-distance relationship, but she felt confident that he was her best match. Scot and Janet visited each other every few months. She liked him, and he seemed to like her and the children well enough. As time passed, things grew serious. Janet was in love. It didn't matter that there were things she didn't like about Scot—after all, everyone has flaws. He was smart, had a good job, owned his own home, and played the cello (beautifully, she might add). And yes, he did have a dog. She was more of a cat person herself, but her family had owned dogs so she could put up with that. And his temper? Everyone gets angry. Janet got angry. Nobody's perfect. It would all work out. What had she heard? *Love conquers all?* Janet believed that Scot was about as perfect a match as she could possibly find anywhere.

15. More Marriage

Scot moved closer so that he could be with Janet. He found a job teaching in a local college. They were getting along well. Janet planned a weekend trip to Nashville, Tennessee; Scot and the two youngest would go with them. It was an exciting place, the home of country music. It seemed everyone there wore cowboy hats and boots. Scot even bought hats and boots for Ella and Cameron. They looked adorable. On their last day, they went to the Grand Ole Opry. They had a special pass to go backstage and look around. As they headed toward the stage door, Scot stopped her. He got down on one knee and asked if she would marry him. Truthfully, Janet had been expecting a proposal for some time. She loved Scot, and thought he'd make a good husband and father, and any fears about their unsuitability were natural. After all, she reminded herself again, this was a new start. No one was perfect. "Yes. *Yes!*" cried Janet. "Of course I'll marry you, Scot." It was four years since her last marriage.

With the impending marriage, Janet's thoughts went to her two older children. Tony, child number one, handled things in stride. After all, he was eighteen and had his whole life in front of him. Janet's pending third marriage didn't seem to bother him. He was working part-time and went to a local university. Scot and Janet had talked about the two older children at great length. What to do with them? Of course, Janet wanted them with her in the five-bedroom house Scot had purchased as their family home, about an hour and a half away from her parents. But Scot wasn't used to all the comings and goings of teenagers. He heartily agreed to take the younger two, but wasn't so sure about the older two. Janet asked Tony and Eva what they would like to do. In the end, after much persuasion on Scot's part, Janet asked her parents if Tony, eighteen, and Eva, sixteen, could live in their basement. And so it was. Part of Janet didn't like the idea—a big part. She and the two older children had been separated enough already, but she didn't want to argue with Scot about it. Anger seemed to rear its ugly head too easily. Anyway, Tony and Eva didn't want to change schools ... they'd done that enough. Janet knew how they felt, because her own dad had been in the army and moved roughly every three years. The two older kids would be fine, Janet told herself. After all, their grandparents were just upstairs and would keep an eye on them. If any problems arose, she would be just over an hour away. Adjusting to this new marriage with Scot and the two younger children would be challenging enough, so wasn't it better if the older two children didn't have to deal with it? Scot, at the ripe age of forty-two, had never been married and was bringing his only "child" Betsy, the mutt, to their family. Deep down, Janet was optimistic. It was all about marrying the right man. What could possibly go wrong? Weren't love, commitment, hopes, and dreams strong enough to weather any problems that could arise? The truth was staring Janet in the face, but because her head was in the sand, she didn't see it.

She and the children moved in with Scot in his home near the town where he was now teaching. The house was away from the main town but close to many shops, so Janet didn't feel like she was in the middle of nowhere, which was something she hated. She had been accepted at the local university. There she would finish her Bachelor of Arts as well as a master's degree in education. For the most part, they all seemed to get along well in the new house. However—there was the dog problem. The kids didn't like that Scot seemingly treated Betsy better and kinder than he treated them. Janet noticed it too. But when she talked to Scot about it, he said they were being ridiculous. Anyway, he said, dogs gave unconditional love to the owners, so they deserved it back. What was wrong with that? One day, Cameron, at the age of fourteen, asked his mother why Scot loved Betsy more than he loved them. She told him that Scot had only lived with pet dogs and never lived with children. Betsy was like his child, and he was doing the best he could. Janet frequently excused Scot's behavior. She didn't want this marriage to end up as divorce number three. But somewhere in the recesses of her mind, she remembered a saying by Maya Angelou:

> *"When someone shows you who they are, believe them the first time."*

16. More Abuse

Another wedding anniversary, Janet mused. Why did they always end up in an enormous fight with her storming off, not wanting to be with Scot for another second longer? Did she need to change something in herself? Was it as he said, that she was selfish and only thought of herself and the kids? Even now, Janet can't remember what the fights were about, only her desperate attempts to get away from him. She had read enough books on marriage and relationships to know that she wasn't the only one to blame and that it takes two to build a loving relationship. She had tried this. In the early days of their marriage, Janet had signed them up for a seminar on love. During the seminar, Scot was uninterested and refused to look at her or follow any of the speaker's instructions for the activity that was designed to build intimacy. Whenever Janet looked at him, his face looked like a storm of anger was brewing and that he might fly out of the building any moment. She also remembered on several occasions, while riding in the car with Scot, she had wanted to jump out and didn't care if the car was moving. All she could hear was a vicious attack of words aimed at her—scathing words that often seemed to come out of nowhere with no provocation. As time went on, Janet learned to give some back. In both her previous marriages, she had this rule: *Be careful what you say, because you can never take it back.* But this marriage brought out all the nastiest words that Janet could find. She wanted to protect herself by throwing hateful words back in order to equal the verbal assaults. As the marriage to Scot was nearing its end, Janet would find herself physically running and hiding from him. Something would start an argument and Scot would get angry, but Janet didn't want to argue. She wanted time and space to sort out her feelings and respond rationally to things he said. And because she didn't want to hear any more angry words, Janet would go into a room and lock the door. She thought she was safe, until Scot began breaking the door down, literally pulling it away from the frame. This happened on several occasions, so the wood on those doors was slightly off the frame. On one occasion, Janet hid from Scot behind the shower curtain in the bathroom. She was scared, so she started to call the police but quickly hung up the phone as she heard Scot approaching. The next thing she knew, the police were at their door. Janet didn't know what to say. Scot made up excuses: "Sorry officers, it was a mistake."

Many times, Janet would drive off in her car late at night and sleep for a few hours in a random parking lot so Scot wouldn't find her to finish the "argument." Eventually, she'd make her way home because she wanted to be there for the kids when they woke up. They seemed none the wiser. Janet was frustrated and scared. Here she was again, wanting out of a marriage. The words that were thrown around in this relationship seemed far more painful than her second husband's words had ever been. How did she end up here again? Why was she so attracted to these unhealthy relationships? Janet knew she needed to get away from Scot, and away from this marriage. It wouldn't be easy, as most of her money was tied up in the family finances and Scot controlled all of those. With her teacher's salary and $45,000 in student loans hanging over her, leaving didn't seem like a very realistic option. Janet was thoroughly miserable. Her mind played out different scenarios. Take the kids and go back to her parents' house? Find a cheap place to rent? Find a job in another state where she could afford to live? Or, when she felt utterly hopeless, she wondered if she should just end her life? She hated to even think this thought, but it had crossed her mind during some low, desperate moments. Janet routinely called her friend Marcy crying because of something Scot had said or done. Marcy told her to leave him, but Janet whined, "It's not that easy. Things are complicated, especially financially..." Marcy told Janet these were all excuses. If she really wanted to leave Scot, she'd find a way.

The years seemed to fly by. The kids were older now, and the thought of leaving Scot filled Janet's every waking moment. As in her previous marriage, Janet knew she had to execute her exodus meticulously. First, she moved into one of the spare bedrooms. Cameron had moved out, so it would just be her and Ella in the house with Scot. Second, she would continue to bring up the topic of divorce to Scot. He seemed to accept the idea, especially when she was told to get the f**k out of his house and take her brats with her.

Janet was working as a teacher. The hours were long but her hope of leaving Scot kept her going. Her mind was always thinking of how she could leave him and still have enough money to live on. Then Janet remembered something from the previous year—a teacher friend had left the school to teach in Europe. Janet asked her friend for the website where she found the job. Having spent eighteen years overseas in her earlier life, Janet was again tired of living in the United States. Perhaps this was the answer to her prayers.

Janet's parents never knew what went on behind closed doors between her and Scot. Whenever they fought, Janet found herself making some excuse to visit with them, without Scot. They seemed none the wiser. She wasn't sure how much the kids knew, but later she found out that they weren't immune to Scot's angry words. She tried not to feel guilty for putting them in this situation. She had done the best she could. Life was short, and Janet wanted better things for herself and her children. She wanted more of the good things in her life. She wanted love, someone to understand her—someone to love her for who she was, not someone who criticized her for who she wasn't. What kind of example was she setting for her children by staying in yet another unhealthy relationship? She bided her time, listened to Oprah, read as many self-help books as she could get her hands on, and began to feel stronger in herself.

17. More Pain

Eva, Janet's oldest girl, was a sweet, motherly child who seemed mature beyond her years. Janet always called upon her to help watch the younger two children. With Janet being a single mother, the extra help Eva provided made Janet's life a bit easier.

When Janet and the two youngest children moved back to the States from England in early 2001, Eva was desperate to join them. She had been living with her brother at the home of their father and his new family, but things were not to her liking. The chance to move to America excited her, so Eva and Tony arranged to leave England that summer. The arrival of the two older children made Janet's family complete. They were all together once again. It was still tough being a single parent, but she did have her own parents for support. Maybe Eva's life would have been different if Janet hadn't married Scot two years later.

The first inkling that there was trouble with Eva was when Janet's mother called to say Eva had not come home from her evening shift at McDonalds. Eva and Tony had been living in the downstairs unit of Janet's parents' home. "Yes, mother." Janet hardened. "I will speak to her." Eva assured

Janet that she would do as her mother asked, but the nights away from home continued. Why wasn't Eva showing the maturity that she possessed? Janet would have never allowed her sixteen-year-old daughter to live with her older brother if she believed her to be irresponsible. Yes, Janet wasn't living in the house with Eva and Tony, but her parents were right upstairs. Couldn't they keep a closer eye on her?

One night, Janet got a frantic call from Eva. She had taken up with a Latino man and was living with his family. The man had become physically abusive. She wanted to leave and come live with Scot and Janet. Janet didn't know exactly where Eva was, but she had a rough idea. It was very dark. Janet said a quick prayer. She eventually found the house, as Eva's old car that Scot and Janet had bought for her was out front. The plan was for Janet to drive Eva back in her car while Scot followed. When Janet knocked on the door, Eva hesitated. Juan had said he was sorry and promised it wouldn't happen again. Janet asked her to come outside to talk. She eventually persuaded Eva to come back with her for the night to think things over. She could always come back here later. Quickly, Janet got Eva in the car and drove off. Eva began to cry, wanting to go back. Janet sped up, not wanting to give her a chance to get out of the car. Suddenly a police siren blared behind them. Janet pulled over and tried to explain to the officer that she needed to get her daughter home. Janet began to cry. The officer asked for the registration, and when Janet reached over to get it from the glovebox, several unpaid speeding tickets fell out. Between sobs, Janet tried to explain that they weren't her tickets. However, the officer had made up his mind: there would be another ticket today. Janet kept an eye on Eva, knowing that the longer they were stopped, the easier it would be for her to get out of the car. By the time the police officer wrote the ticket, Janet was hysterical. He told her to calm down because he wouldn't let her drive in that state. Janet tried, but she couldn't calm herself. It seemed as if years of pain and worry were surfacing right here in this moment. The officer walked to Scot's car, who had been parked behind, and told him that Janet must stop crying and be calm before he would let her drive, and if she didn't stop, the car would be impounded. That seemed to sober Janet up, and she calmed herself enough to drive home. Eva stayed with Janet that night, but when Janet came home from work the next day, Eva was gone. Janet's mind was filled with guilt. Perhaps if she and Scot had allowed Eva to live with them in the beginning, this would have never happened. Why did Eva think it was ok for a man to beat her? Hadn't Janet taught her anything?

Janet knew she had to get Eva away from this abusive man. Eva wasn't attending her high school classes and was in danger of not graduating. Then another call came. Eva had not been to school in a week and the school would have to report it to the authorities. Janet rang Eva's friends, one of whom told her that she and Juan had moved into the city and were living in one of the housing developments there. The friend had a vague idea where and gave Janet the name of the neighborhood. Janet had to find her. She told Scot they needed to move fast. They would begin to look for Eva using the tiny bit of information they had. If they could locate Eva's car, they'd know they were at the right place. It was daylight by now, and they drove around several streets before Janet noticed it. There was Eva's car, with the windscreen smashed in. Was Eva ok? Had she been in an accident? They rang the bell, not knowing what to expect. A surprised Eva answered the door. No, Juan was not there. Eva led Janet into the living room. In all her life, Janet had never seen such squalor. She had to keep her composure for Eva's sake, and diverted the conversation to the car. Juan had gotten mad and smashed it, Eva said. Was Eva ok? Yes. He took his anger out on the car this time. Janet wasn't sure Eva was telling the truth—after all, Juan had hit her before. There was an air of urgency as Juan could be back any minute. Janet told Eva that she needed to come back with them, and that she was jeopardizing her future by not going to school. Graduation was only a few months away!

A few days later, Janet and Eva visited the high school to see if Eva could take some online classes. The semester was almost over, and she hadn't completed enough work to meet the requirements for graduation. Over the next few weeks, Janet encouraged Eva to finish the courses. She had moved back to her grandparents and felt much happier there. And although Janet tried to monitor Eva's comings and goings, it was difficult because Eva had her own car. She needed one, of course, to get to school and work (at least that's what Janet told herself).

It was about a week before her graduation. Eva had a bruise that stretched the length of her entire forearm, so Janet knew that Eva had been seeing Juan again. Eva told her that Juan had gotten into one of his tempers and beat her. Janet pleaded with her to go to the police and report him, and then asked Eva why she thought she deserved his beating. Eva was silent. Eventually, she did go to the police. Unfortunately, in every graduation photo, even when she was smiling happily, the bruise was there. What about the bruises on Eva's heart? Janet was a strong woman and thought she had raised Eva to be strong as well. Why, oh why, did she allow him to beat her? Janet struggled with the reasons, and even spoke to one of the female police officers about it. Why would a woman go back to a man who beat her? Was there anything that she as a mother could do to help Eva? The officer wisely explained, "No one can help her until she's ready to help herself. And unfortunately," she concluded, "Eva will most likely keep going back to him." Janet believed going to the police was the first step toward Eva's healing (or so she thought), until she found out that it was Eva who had given Juan a ride to his court appearance.

After graduation, Eva appeared to be staying away from Juan, despite having driven him to court. She started working part-time but couldn't settle into any one job. Then she came home with big news: she was joining the Marines. Excitement oozed from every pore as she spoke, but all Janet could ask was, "Why the Marines?" Eva explained, "They have the reputation of being one of the toughest branches in the

US military. The Marines are usually the first to be sent into a battle zone." Eva maintained that she wanted to be the best version of herself, and the recruitment officer bragged that joining the Marines was the only way to do that.

Janet wanted to give Eva her opportunity to shine. Besides that, it wouldn't hurt for her to be as far away from Juan as she could possibly be. A few weeks later Eva was on her way to Parris Island, South Carolina. Boot camp wouldn't be that bad, as it was winter. The mosquitoes weren't due out in swarms until early spring. Unbeknownst to Janet, after Eva's high school graduation, she had taken up with another Latino man, Alfonso. While at boot camp, Eva left Janet in charge of her phone. A man called regularly and left several messages of how he loved and missed Eva. Janet was tempted to answer and say, "You can't have her. She's out getting trained to kick your ass." Janet hoped Eva would be too busy to think about him. The Marines would help her become the woman she was meant to be. And never again would she let any man abuse her, reasoned Janet.

The day of boot camp graduation arrived. No one in the family had seen Eva for twelve weeks. Janet wasn't sure what to expect, but she went along with her parents and Eva's three siblings for the four-and-a-half hour drive. They almost didn't recognize Eva. She was trim and looking smart in her uniform. She walked confidently as she showed them many of the difficult tasks that she had learned to accomplish. Everyone was so proud of her. Things were finally beginning to look up for Eva, mused Janet.

After boot camp, Eva was given a couple of weeks of leave. She decided she wanted to stay with Janet and Scot. They didn't actually see much of her, as she spent most of the time visiting friends. As the leave period ended, Eva seemed excited and happy about joining the rest of her fellow Marines at Camp LeJeune.

Janet believed in God, and always thought He would only give her what she could handle. But often, what one thinks they can handle is somewhat skewed towards the reality of what lies ahead.

About a month after Eva left for Camp LeJeune, Janet received a call from an officer informing her that Eva had gone AWOL (Absent Without Official Leave). "Do you know where Eva is? If so," he made clear, "you should urge her to return to base or she could face time in prison." The news sickened Janet. How in the world could Eva have left the camp? New recruits were supposed to be on a tight leash, having just graduated boot camp. A few days later the county sheriff paid Janet a visit, inquiring about her daughter's whereabouts. Janet swore she had no idea where Eva was, and realized the seriousness of the situation.

Janet told her parents what happened and that she needed to find Eva. Her first line of inquiry began with a search for any friend that might know of Eva's whereabouts. From that, Janet learned the approximate location, so she drove there and started knocking on doors. It took a few doors, but eventually someone offered some information. Janet knew she had to plan things carefully. She spoke with her mother who agreed to help Janet find Eva. They would locate the house, get Eva, and drive her back to the Marine camp. Janet and her mother arrived at the suspected house around four in the morning. The information they had gotten suggested they come early. The neighbor had told Janet that people were coming and going to work at that time. Janet's mom would stay with the car while Janet approached the house. She knocked on the front door and said Eva's name. The person who answered was Hispanic and Janet wasn't sure how much English he understood, but when he heard the name "Eva," he pointed to the back of the house. Janet went around the back and knocked on the door. Through a window, she could see someone sleeping on the couch. As she knocked again, the person got up and came to the door. Janet said Eva's name again. The man who was sleeping on the sofa went and knocked on another bedroom door, and a moment later, out came a groggy Eva. Janet told her to get her things. They needed to go now, or she would be committing a felony and most likely be put in jail. At that point, Eva's Hispanic boyfriend came out and started arguing. "Eva won't get into trouble. She can do what she wants. Get out of here!" he barked. Janet was furious. "How dare you! The Marines do not take running away lightly. Eva will end up in jail!" *What did he know about the Marines anyway,* she hissed to herself. Janet ignored his arguments, and after ten minutes she finally persuaded Eva to come with her. Janet wasted no time and bundled Eva into the car. She would take over the driving now. They sped off towards Camp LeJeune. Having a captive audience, Janet and her mother tried to speak kindly to Eva about the consequences. They were assured by the powers that be that it would be better if Eva turned herself in as opposed to the Marines coming to find her. The drive was a long, anxiety-filled four hours. Once they reached the camp, they were directed to an office. No time was wasted. As soon as the officer in charge saw Eva, he ranted and raved like a madman. An exhausted, scared Eva stood at attention. The tirade went on for what seemed like hours. Janet and her mom sat, frozen, feeling Eva's discomfort, but they both knew this was the military's way of dealing with a problem of such seriousness. When the harangue ended, Eva was escorted toward the sleeping quarters. She would be confined to the base with no use of a cell phone. Janet and her mother gave her a quick hug. They felt some relief that she had gotten off so lightly and headed back up north.

Roughly two weeks went by when Janet received another call. "Eva has gone AWOL again, and this time she will be charged *when,* not if, she is found," the officer thundered. Janet was beside herself with the bad news. *Eva, what have you done, you silly, stupid girl?* As a mother, Janet had to ask herself what part she had played in Eva's troubles. Should she have made Eva come live with her and Scot from the start? Maybe she shouldn't have given her access to a car? What else could she have done to prevent this mess? Her eldest daughter was going to end up in jail. What kind of life would she have with that on her record? Once again, the county sheriff came to visit Janet, only this time he had a warrant for Eva's arrest. He politely stated, "If you or anyone else knows where Eva is located, you need to turn her in." More questions raced through Janet's mind: *How in the hell did she get away from the camp? She didn't have a cell phone. Why did she leave again, knowing the seriousness of the consequences?*

The next few months were difficult for Janet. She was doing her student teaching and finishing her teaching degree. Not knowing where or how Eva was consumed her thoughts. Janet was crying a lot more. She was still taking antidepressants, but the heartache and worry she felt seemed to override the effectiveness of the pills. Later, Janet found out that someone in the camp had let Eva use their phone. Eva had contacted her boyfriend, who then drove to the camp to pick her up. The months dragged by, and Janet used every ounce of strength she had within herself to keep her life normal, taking care of the other children, dealing with household needs, and keeping up with her studies, all the while student teaching. Then out of the blue, Janet got a message from Eva's dad. She had somehow made her way to England. But that wasn't all. Janet held her breath ... Eva was pregnant! He would be sending her back with her older brother, Tony, who happened to be visiting him at the time. Janet's emotions were a whirlwind. She couldn't wait to see Eva, and her heart flooded with relief that she was coming back! But that flood of emotion soon turned to trepidation in light of what Eva's future might hold.

When the day came, Janet and the two youngest children were waiting at the international arrivals area of the airport.

They saw Tony, but Eva was nowhere to be found. Somberly, Tony recounted what had happened. When the plane landed, before the passengers were released, two men had boarded the plane. They called out Eva's name to the seated passengers. They insisted that she make herself known to them. She did, and they escorted her off the plane. Tony had asked what would happen to her, to which the officers only replied that they would be in touch soon. The relief Janet felt receded briskly. What would happen to her now?

Soon, an update came by phone: Eva was on camp arrest on a Marine camp in California. She told Janet that the day she and Tony landed, she was transferred straight away onto a plane bound for California. The guards handcuffed her and sat on either side of her for the entire five-hour plane ride. They wouldn't even unlock the cuffs for her to use the bathroom, as she was a flight risk. Janet told Eva she would do whatever it took to fly to California to see her.

While on camp arrest, Eva worked as a clerk until the powers that be decided her fate: court-martial and prison, or dishonorable discharge. Janet only had a few days with Eva, but she seemed to accept her fate, whatever that would be. Eva had plenty of undisturbed time to think about her actions. During one of their heart-to-heart talks, Eva confided in Janet. Had she not been pregnant, she would have liked to stay in the Marines, if that was even an option for a deserter. One thing Eva did know for certain was that she did not want to be a single mother. Janet flew back to North Carolina.

18. More Life

In time, Eva was dismissed from the Marines with a less-than-honourable discharge. It turned out to be a blessing, as she would otherwise have a prison record. Janet thought that Eva would come and stay with her and Scot until she figured things out, but she disappeared again. For months, Janet heard nothing from her. What could she do but wait and hope that Eva would contact her? The baby must be due soon. Sure enough, Janet received the long-awaited phone call. "Yes, I am fine, Mom. Yes, the baby is fine, due in three weeks. Where am I? Edinburgh, Scotland. No, I'm not alone. Alfonso, the father, is with me." Janet wondered how much more of this she could take. Alfonso was the one who got her into trouble with the Marines in the first place. What the hell was Eva doing with him? Janet didn't think he was the kind of guy who would treat Eva kindly, not if her short argumentative interaction with him was anything to go by. Janet decided she would go to see Eva once the baby was born.

Annie was an adorable baby who filled everyone's hearts with joy. Janet had arrived in Scotland when Annie was only a few weeks old. She really tried to get along with Alfonso, but he seemed to be an odious, self-serving individual who wanted to control everyone and everything. He actually forbade Janet from visiting her daughter and granddaughter. Of course, Janet wasn't going to take orders from Alfonso, and she came and went as she pleased and totally ignored him when he was there. She had hoped that the birth of their child might help soften him and make him appreciate Eva's hard work as a mother and wife, but it had the opposite effect. Truthfully, Janet didn't care if Alfonso liked her or not. Eva and Annie were her only concern. Needless to say, Janet's time with Eva and the baby was short. As Janet left them to return home, she thought the only thing she could do was pray that God would help Eva and that one day her oldest daughter would find a better life for herself.

19. More Time

Things with Scot had not improved. Maybe it didn't help that Janet stayed in one of the spare bedrooms and rarely talked to him, or that she started chatting to men online to distract herself from the pain she felt every day in the marriage. Janet continually asked herself: *When will you leave him? Will there ever be a right time to leave?* Surrounding herself with self-help books, Janet constantly filled her mind with ideas about how to get what you want, how to heal, how to be your best self, how to be the love you want, how to live your dreams, and so on. As she focused on these notions, Janet's heart began to fill with hope.

20. More Divorce

Finally, the divorce was finished. Janet didn't contest it as it would mean that she would have to stay in contact with Scot, something she balked at. Did it matter that she was left with nothing but $45,000 in student loan debt ... debt that he helped her acquire? Or did it matter that she was seemingly not entitled to share any equity in their marital home ... equity which she contributed to? If Janet had been paying attention over the years, she would have seen it. She took the easy road. She stayed ignorant where money was concerned and gave her power away. How many times had Scot remortgaged their home? She didn't understand all that was involved. She just blindly signed the papers. Janet tried to remember the good times they had together, but there seemed to be so many awful ones that the good ones were hard to find. She was amazed that she lasted this long. The warning signs were there; she just chose to ignore them. Why is it that women think men will change, or behave differently or better once they get married? Janet didn't purposely set out to change Scot—she just thought it would happen automatically. How wrong she was to think she could change someone. She believed his love for her would make him want to be a better person. Janet's children were tired of all the anger and tension, so they were in favor of the divorce. They had all gone their separate ways by then, but they told Janet later that Scot had spoken very harshly towards them when she wasn't around. When Ella was sixteen, she had run away, apparently the result of something Scot had said to her. Janet had gone to Scotland to see Eva after Annie was born. On arriving back home, Ella was gone. Scot had some excuse about headstrong teenage girls. Nevertheless, Ella had never run away while Janet was there. Once again, with a heavy heart, Janet went out to search for one of her daughters. The angels seemed to be with her, as Janet had acquired enough information and was able to track down Ella quickly. Now time had passed, and Ella and Cameron had moved out. This was the sign Janet needed to leave Scot and the home she had known for the past eleven years.

21. More Adventures

August 2013

Having never been to the Middle East, Janet was taken with the bold, symmetrical, and remarkable architecture she encountered there. Every direction she looked confirmed that she was no longer in the West, and she loved it! Her job provided her a good salary, housing, and money to rent a car. Janet needed a car. So what if the locals drove crazy and didn't seem to follow any real traffic rules? She could hold her own on the roads. The school was an interesting set up. It would take some getting used to, but what she loved most was that they didn't require much paperwork when dealing with the students. No paperwork! It was worth the move for that reason alone! Janet loved teaching and hoped this move would give her the chance to be the teacher she always dreamed of being. She had already made friends with two other teachers from New Zealand. Janet preferred being around non-Americans, as she felt embarrassed by how they always managed to complain about how things "weren't like this" back home. Janet became close friends with one of the New Zealanders, Jana, who was gorgeous and had a good eye for fashion. With Jana's help, Janet was able to recreate herself into a stylish and sexier version. Janet couldn't believe it was her when she caught a glimpse of herself in the mirror.

She felt freer in the Middle East than she had ever felt before, as this would be the first time in her life that Janet lived on her own. She was like a young woman again, one who had been given another chance at life. She was still in contact with Tim, but because she only knew him by photos and texts, Janet decided it was time to meet a man in person—a dark, handsome Arab, or an expatriate, British preferably. When she was ready for a date, with Jana's help, as well as her own hardy exercise routine, Janet looked very, very attractive, even at fifty years old. Many of the men here seemed to prefer blonde ladies, so she took advantage of this. Within months of arriving in Dubai, Janet had lots of offers. Janet was using a dating app that Jana had recommended, but she didn't want to rush into anything. Marriage was the past. She was ready for fun!

22. More Knowledge, More Wisdom, More Love

In her new home, Janet continued to fill her shelves with self-help books, which she studied routinely. The last one she read encouraged her to be the person she was looking for in her life, and not to look outside of herself for love. If she didn't truly love herself, she wouldn't know how to truly love or attract the right kind of person. In Janet's heart of hearts, she wanted to be loved and she knew she deserved it. The time had come to not settle for anything less than what she deserved. If her three marriages had taught her anything, they taught her the things she *didn't* want in a relationship. And it was better to be alone and lonely than in a relationship and lonely. All she needed now was to focus on what she did want. Janet wrote down the qualities she wanted in her next relationship. It seemed like a 'pie in the sky' shopping list, but she knew if she wanted it, she had to believe and stay focused on it.

Six months later, Janet had three dates lined up in a single week. The first one was a middle-aged British ex-army man, the second was a Moroccan (the youngest of the three), and the last was an Emirati. It's funny how life shows you things you want but you have to actually recognize them and make a decision to take them. The British man took her to an average restaurant. They talked for hours about things and seemed to have much in common. He was even in Germany at the same time as Janet many years before. Despite this, as the dinner came to an end, Janet knew she wouldn't be seeing him again. He talked too much about his grandchildren, and even though by that time Janet had a couple grandchildren herself, it made her feel old and she didn't want that. The next day, her date was with a young and very handsome Moroccan guy who was in the army. They met at a local coffee shop. Janet was immediately attracted to him. He was funny and charming and although his English needed some practice, he made her laugh. They seemed to laugh the whole time. As the evening ended, Janet drove him back to his accommodation. She hoped he had felt the same attraction that she did. Two days later, Janet had her third date, this time with the Emirati man. They too met in a coffee shop, where he regaled her with stories of his time in England. He was a pilot, divorced, with a disabled mother at home. Janet enjoyed their conversation but was still reminiscing about her time with the young, handsome Moroccan man a few evenings before. As the time ended with date number three, he asked if he could call her. Maybe they could go out again? Janet agreed, though somewhat reluctantly. He was pleasant enough to be with, and closer to her age ... maybe she should give him a chance? Wasn't that a wise thing to do? The next evening, he called. He wanted to see Janet again soon. But

Janet had been texting Hassan, the Moroccan, throughout most of the day. She really liked Hassan, even though he was half her age. "I'm sorry, I'm busy," Janet lied. She had no interest in seeing anyone but Hassan. She mentioned her three dates to one of the teachers and told her how she was attracted to the youngest of them. The teacher sneered, "Just stick to your own age group. You have nothing in common with him." Janet insisted, "But he makes me laugh. And how do you know what we have in common?" This was a rare opportunity, and Janet wasn't going to listen to advice just because someone thought they knew what was best for her. Janet's heart told her to choose Hassan. There was something about him.

23. More Happiness

Janet and Hassan spent as much time together as they possibly could. They went to concerts, ate at restaurants, played sports, and rode bikes. Sometimes Janet cooked for Hassan and sometimes he cooked for her. And they laughed. Janet didn't plan to fall in love with Hassan. After all, there was the age difference. But out here, age didn't seem to be an issue. Hassan didn't give it a second thought. And if that was her only concern, why should it matter? It was her life. Janet held back telling Hassan how she felt. She wanted to gauge his feelings. Two months later, it came. Sent first by text, then spoken. He loved her. Janet couldn't believe it! And then she deliberated. *Why not?* For months Janet and Hassan had been spending almost every day together. They had so much fun and seemed to be in sync. Sometimes, they even said what the other was thinking or finished each other's sentences. And Hassan was so kind, so very kind and loving. Janet never had a man in her life treat her or speak to her like he did. She marveled at it all, especially when she found the list that she had written down months before with the qualities she wanted in her next relationship—it described Hassan perfectly! As Janet reflected back to those three dates and the slight hesitancy to forget Hassan because of his age, she knew things could have turned out very differently if she had listened to reason. She would have missed the greatest love of her life, the partner of her soul, Hassan. Thank God she had listened to her heart.

24. More Heartache of a Different Kind

Janet and Hassan had been together almost three years when Janet received the worst phone call of her life. It happened around ten o'clock in the evening. It was Ella, and she was sobbing. Cameron was dead! Janet was stunned. Did she hear that right? Cameron was dead? Ella didn't know any of the details and could hardly speak. The shockwaves spread quickly throughout Janet's body. She couldn't think clearly. Then her motherly instincts kicked in. She had to get back to her children—back on the next plane to the States. It would take over fourteen hours, but she had to do it.

Janet sobbed silently for most of the plane ride. She had a lot of time to come to grips with the news. Ella met her at the airport. They fell into each other's arms, each crying loudly. They didn't care—the pain was unbearable. On the ride back from the airport, Ella told Janet that the sheriff's office had given her a number to call to find out more details of Cameron's death. That night, Janet and Ella met Tony at a local fast-food place. They grabbed a quick bite, although none of them were very hungry. Tony told them that Eva would fly in from Scotland the next evening, and that she and Janet could stay in his trailer for the night to make things easier, as it was close to the sheriff's office. The next day, Janet called the number that had been given to them. She and Ella could go to speak with the investigating officer in person. The sheriff's building was not much bigger than a trailer itself, with a small waiting room inside the front door and two internal windows at which to request an officer. They came out quickly and said how sorry they were for their loss. Janet and Ella had been crying in the car on the way over, but Janet knew she had to control herself in order to ask the questions and get answers. "What happened?" she stammered. As best they could tell, the assailant went into the laundry mat where Cameron was doing his laundry and shot him point-blank in the face. "Can I see him?" Janet whimpered. Ella sat sobbing beside her. "His body has been sent up North for fingerprint identification. That's the only way they can identify him because of where he was shot." She couldn't believe what she was hearing. "You mean he can't be identified because his face has been blown off?" groaned Janet. "He didn't suffer, in case you were wondering," the officer broke in. "But we and the coroner strongly advise against viewing his body. It would be very traumatic," they cautioned. By the time this information was relayed to Janet and Ella, their wails and sobs had filled the tiny waiting room. Janet was trying to make sense of what she had just heard. Cameron, her youngest child, was brutally murdered? Cameron, that loving man, father of a young daughter whom he adored. A guy who would do anything for anyone he cared about. The same guy that had worked in an orphanage while he was stationed in Korea. Who would want to murder him in such a brutal way?

Janet and Ella were given the name of the funeral parlor where Cameron's body would be transferred to once he was identified. Janet had only a short time to put things in order. The officer's words were spinning constantly in her mind. She couldn't stop crying. Everywhere she went, she sobbed like there was no tomorrow. She didn't care what people thought. Even in the grocery store, when the tears welled up, she let them cascade down her face. If she became overwhelmed by the sorrow, she would go to a corner to try to stifle her sobs.

So much to do and organize. Janet contacted one of her friends, whose son had been a good friend of Cameron's. She asked her to organize a memorial service of some kind—not in the church. Janet couldn't stand the hypocrisy of the church at this moment in time.

Cameron had been living in his car, working all the hours God sent and paying child support to take care of his three-year-old daughter. He couldn't afford to rent a place. He didn't seem to mind living in his car, as long as he could spend time with his daughter. The child's mother had left him for someone else, but Cameron wasn't going to shirk any responsibility for Eleanor's upkeep. Three months earlier, while still in Dubai, Janet had contacted a church in the States. She hated the thought of Cameron spending the holidays in his car, especially with it being winter. She called the office of the church she had attended some years before. She explained Cameron's housing problem, and the lady said the pastor would get back to her. After some time with no reply, Janet called again. She begged the lady for permission for her son to live in the church. "There must be some room he could sleep in." Janet was sure he could help clean the building if they only let him sleep there. "Couldn't the pastor make an announcement and ask if anyone could put him up?" Janet pleaded. The lady informed Janet that she had given the pastor her message, but he was wary of asking his congregation to house people he didn't know. "But we used to attend services there," Janet explained. "My mother and father went there, too." The kind lady said she would leave another message with the pastor.

Janet knew that she shouldn't blame them for what happened to Cameron. But she wanted to blame someone, someone besides the murderer who took Cameron's life. And the guilt! She didn't expect the flood of guilt that came. She knew if she was going to get through all of this, she would have to rise above these heavy feelings.

Janet and Ella made the agonizing trip to the funeral parlor. Ella sobbed and sobbed while Janet and the funeral director sorted out Cameron's death certificate and the cause of death. Janet's broken heart wanted to join Ella's sobs, but she stifled them in order to get through all of the paperwork required. As she spoke with the director, he too recommended a non-viewing of Cameron's body. Cremation might be a better choice than burial. They agreed. Cameron's ashes would be divided into four containers, one for each of them. The funeral director would supply the necessary paperwork so Janet and Eva could travel outside the United States with Cameron's ashes. Since his body was not due back until the end of the week, Janet decided to have the memorial service for him first.

Janet's younger brother traveled up to be there for her. She was numb with pain and had trouble making simple decisions. She, Ella, and Eva had to move out of their hotel room. Janet didn't know where they would go. Her brother, Eddy, came to the rescue; he graciously paid for a hotel suite for the three of them. The memorial service was in a few hours, and Janet's friend had secured a room in a local restaurant.

Janet's father and older sister were there. She only expected half a dozen people or so, but the room was full of friends and workmates who wanted to pay tribute to Cameron's life. It was all a blur. Tears, tears, so many tears, pictures of Cameron on a board, a book being passed around in which to write about Cameron, a painting. Kind words, a toast to Cameron's life by his best friend, Cameron's workmates chatting, a secret toast of whiskey in the back of a van, Cameron's favorite songs filling the air, his precious daughter Eleanor, rain, so much rain, a storm, a woman who said she loved Cameron.

25. More Journeys

Arriving at the airport, Janet couldn't speak without sobbing. She carried Cameron's ashes in her carry-on bag, paperwork in hand. "Madam, what is in the container?" the airport security officer asked politely. Janet broke down, heaving with pain. The words wouldn't come out. She showed him the paperwork and wailed. Other passengers stared, and someone offered her tissues. It was as if the pain came from another realm. Janet didn't know what to do with it or how to control it. Another long flight, only this time she had the facts of Cameron's death, his violent murder, to fill her thoughts.

The long flight over, and again the questions: "What is this, madam?" Again, the uncontrollable sobbing. Nothing in Janet's life had prepared her for this. The tears subsided momentarily as she managed to hail a taxi. Life would be so much different from now on.

26. Epilogue: More Remembering

It has been two years since Cameron's murder, and the dull ache in Janet's soul has never subsided. Tears come at unsuspecting moments. What does she really know about grief and how to live with it? The only thing Janet does know is that in her heart of hearts, Cameron is in a better place, a happier place, watching over them. Ella even has dreams about him, in which he's his same old smart-aleck self. Eva is angry, so angry that his life was cut short in such a brutal way. Tony doesn't say much. He and Cameron were as close as any two brothers could be, and the pain of Cameron's absence is always with him. When Janet was last in Edinburgh, she donated money to a charity that helps people remember loved ones by putting a plaque on a tree somewhere in the city with words about the lost loved one. Janet found a mighty oak tree in a quiet park that was available. Eva goes there periodically and says it's a grand giant of a tree, perfect for Cameron's memory. None of the other family members have visited it but they hope to the next time they are in Edinburgh. Janet anticipates taking Eleanor, Cameron's daughter, there one day to see the tree with the plaque on it in remembrance of her father. She wants to share with Eleanor the city that he loved and tell her how much her dad loved and adored her.

27. More True Love

In Janet's search for something more, life gave her many things she hadn't wished for. But in order to challenge their arrival, Janet recognized that she had to first question her beliefs about herself, especially when her own verbal self-abuse was worse than any she had attracted in her past relationships. Yet, despite knowing all of this, Janet clung to her desire for more love—true love. And in the end, she didn't settle for anything less.

Janet is still in Dubai and still with the partner of her soul, Hassan. His love for her is everything she ever dreamed of and so much more. Every day they spend together, he shows her more beauty, more laughter, more love. Janet admits that the path she took to find Hassan was indeed painfully slow and rocky, but she wouldn't have traded it for the world. She doesn't know what the future holds for her, or for them, but Janet discovered that she could choose. She could choose more, and there is always more!

28. Questions of More

As we caught glimpses into Janet's life and the problems she encountered, we may have recognized something of ourselves in them. Would we have done anything differently than Janet? Perhaps if Janet had done this, or not done that, then this or that would have never happened? If only she had waited, then _____________ might not have taken place. It's easy to look at another person's life and have all the answers. We may even ask ourselves the same questions:

- How did I end up in this place?
- Why do I keep making the same mistakes?
- Are my thoughts creating my reality?
- When will I get it right?
- What do I want out of this life?
- Is there ever a right time to leave a bad relationship?
- Who am I really?
- How can I get more of the life I truly desire?

We have but one life; one life to live the best that we possibly can. If we aren't happy with what we have, then we must search and ask those difficult questions of how we got to where we are. The truth is out there. May we all find it and live a life of more—more of the good that we desire.

29. More Help and Information

B ooks from Janet's Library:

1. *Enchanted Love*, Marianne Williamson
2. *A Return to Love*, Marianne Williamson
3. *Feel the Fear and Do it Anyway*, Susan Jeffers
4. *A Road Less Traveled*, Scott M. Peck
5. *I Declare*, Joel Osteen
6. *Healing Words*, Larry Dossey
7. *Anatomy of the Spirit*, Caroline Myss, Ph.D.
8. *Mirror Work*, Louise Hay
9. *Manifest Your Destiny*, Wayne Dyer
10. *Forgiveness*, Iyanla Vanzant
11. *In the Meantime*, Iyanla Vanzant
12. *Simple Abundance*, Sarah Ban Breathnach
13. *Something More*, Sarah Ban Breathnach
14. *Letting Go*, David R. Hawkins MD., PhD.
15. *The Untethered Soul*, Michael A. Singer
16. *The Secret*, Rhonda Byrne
17. *The Magic*, Rhonda Byrne
18. *Quantum Love*, Laura Berman, PhD.

Inside A Life of More

More Money

20 May 2013

Dear Janet's Better Half (the real me ☺),

Why, oh why has it taken me 50 years to figure things out?! I read a lot about living a good life and how to have the perfect relationship, but I had never heard this before: "Every choice you make is either from a place of fear or love". The pastor had said it last Sunday. It was something I needed to think about and reflect on – especially since my life seems such a mess at this point. I have to figure out where I'm going wrong so I don't keep hating the life I am currently living. Well, I know one thing – I am choosing love – love for myself. And the life I live will be on my terms without anyone else telling me what to do. This teaching job in Dubai will help me get away from number 3 and any negative influences. And the money! Any that I earn will be all mine!! I can spend as I like, minus the lectures and guilt trips. And one of the most exciting parts, I will be alone for the first time in my adult life!! How long have I waited for this? 30 years at least? Xx

More Questions

25 May 2013

Dear Janet's Better Half,

As I have been reflecting on my life and the decisions I've made, I've come to the conclusion that I always seem to be seeking something more: more love, more money, more happiness, more life. I admit that I've rushed into many a life decision, but the bottom line was I was looking for more. I still have many questions though: How did I get to this place in my life? Why did I, do I keep making the same mistakes? When will I get it right?!! Who the hell is Janet really? And most importantly: what is my life for and what do I want to do with it?

I am guilty of ignoring my intuition, you know, that little voice that says, "wait" or "don't do it, don't marry him." And the price for ignoring it – PAIN! Pure unadulterated PAIN!!!! Not only for me, but for my four babies. Sometimes I wish they had a mother that could make good decisions, for everyone's sake. How many times did I wish, especially in my marriages that I could turn the clock back and unmarry. Okay, that's not a word, but that's what I wanted. And as I continue my search for love, the partner of my soul, I find myself rushing into my next relationship before this one is even cold in its grave! Wake up woman! Could that be the problem? How do I know what I want in a relationship? Have I ever really given it much thought? Much time? I know it's an avoidance technique. "Avoid the pain at all costs." My mind yells, but my heart says "Wait. Heal. Think."

2 June 2013

Hello Better Half,

I love you. That's what I am supposed to say as I look in the mirror each morning, but you know what? It's sooooooo hard! Why can't I say it and mean it? Could it be that I've spent most of my life hating myself and this body I am in? It's not going to change in a few weeks what I have been practicing my whole life, this negative self-talk. Anyway, I am willing to give it a go. Who knows? Maybe it will bring good things into my life if I can truly love myself.

10 June 2013

I found one of my journals from when I was 14. How grown-up I thought I was. It always gives me a good laugh to read it. In fact, sometimes I feel like I am still a teenager.

More Youth

4 November 1977

I think I heard the voice of God. I was reading my bible and I saw it. It said go back to the home of your fathers. I am interested in missionary work. Could it be that my calling is to Scotland? That's where many of my ancestors came from, plus they have cool things like the bagpipes and kilts. I'll keep asking God.

8 November 1977

Happy 14th birthday to me! Sometimes I feel very sad and don't have a reason. Although I have my whole future to look forward to. It's Prince Charles birthday next week. He'll be 30. Gosh that's old. I told Marcy that I want to celebrate his birthday during lunch time.

12 November 1977

I think I got confirmation of my answer: The Black Watch are coming to the Arena for a concert. I told mom that I wanted to go and would do anything she wanted me to just so I could go. She said yes. Hallelujah!!

4 December 1977

Wow! What a night! That's it, I am going to Scotland. Especially if the men look like Andy. He was one of the sword dancers. I bought a record and during the intermission I saw him standing there so I asked him to sign it. I think I'm in love. I got his picture too.

More World

5 October 1980

There was a missionary at church today and he works in Scotland! He's single. I spoke to him and invited him over for dinner. Mom doesn't care. Can't wait, can't wait, can't wait!!!!

6 October 1980

That's it. I'm going to Scotland. I had a great time at dinner picking Archie's brain. He gave me his address in Scotland and the mission board he is with. All I have to do is contact them and tell them I'm interested in going for the summer. He may not be back then but there are others I can stay and work with. I can't believe it's happening. Every night, when I kiss Andy's picture goodnight (he's soooooo handsome in his Black Watch kilt), I pray to God that I can go and maybe even meet Andy when I'm in Scotland. So, so excited!!!

8 November 1980

Happy 17th to me. I told mom that I want a ticket to Scotland for my birthday, Christmas, and graduation. I like the US, but I want to see more of the world. I have to go. I've told everyone I'm going.

12 February 1981

I got my plane ticket!!!! I fly into Prestwick on May 27. When I wrote to the mission board they didn't know who I was, but I got Archie and someone at church to write me a reference. I'm almost there!

27 May 1981

I got picked up in a tiny car with a big man driving. I didn't talk much. I think I was trying to take it all in. So green, everywhere I look. Also, scary driving on the other side of the road. What's that smell?

I asked the driver– the Brewery. It's divine. Edinburgh is very nice. Lots of old buildings, but they are dirty looking. Rain heavy rain.

28 May 1981

I'm staying in a big house with three floors. I'm in the middle, all to myself. The missionary couple is on the top floor and the office is on the bottom floor. I met Sam today. He actually wouldn't leave me alone. He started teasing me because I was American. I have to work in the office with him. Not sure I'll enjoy it.

29 May 1981

Well that guy Sam is being a pain. He follows me around and wants me to walk around the city with him. He looks older than me. We had an argument today. I told him that I liked the Scottish accent. He told me I was the one with the accent. I said I wasn't because I was American. He laughed and then kept laughing. Then he got really serious and said he couldn't have an accent because it was his country. And how dare I think otherwise. I don't like him.

30 May 1981

I had the day off. Sam came over and took me on the double decker bus. I said yes because there was no one else. I loved the bus ride. We sat up in the top on the very first seat. I thought we were going to crash into the bus in front of us. I still don't like Sam. He told me that God told him I am to be his wife. I said God hadn't told me that so he could leave me out of it. I don't know. He's not bad looking just a bit pushy.

1 June 1981

Had a good day. Sam showed me a duck pond just down the road. He keeps asking me things, mainly about what I believe. I think he just likes to argue. Oh well, I don't have to answer him do I? I did let him buy me fish and chips. They were the most delicious things ever. The guy wrapped them in newspaper, which I thought was funny. And then it began to rain. We ran to a bus stop for shelter and managed to eat before we got soaked through. The sun was down by then so the rain felt cold even though it's summer. Sam walked me back to the place I am staying.

8 June 1981

I'm off to the Borders. Sam says it's the place where Scotland has to touch England. I thought that was a funny thing to say. Weren't they one country after all? He got really quiet and then said I had better not be saying things like that in Scotland or I might get a Glaswegian kiss. I told him I didn't want a kiss from anyone. He then told me what it really was. Someone bashes their head against yours. Ouch! Must remember: Scottish people don't like the English.

10 June 1981

I feel like I'm a million miles away from civilization down here, but I really like this family. The dad is funny and the mom doesn't take anything seriously. The kids are sweet too. They told me they have a surprise for me tomorrow. Can't imagine what it is. We have to be up early for it.

11 June 1981

What a day! We all piled into their car and we went up north to Loch Lomond. It took hours, but the scenery was beautiful and green. And Mr. B let me drive. I was scared but I didn't want him to think I didn't know how so I switched places with him. There were a couple of problems. I don't know how to drive a stick shift and the roads were tiny, with room for only one car. But I wanted to try. It was ok until I stalled the car and then saw another car heading...

to be continued...

For more information about the author, visit:
N. Lynn's website: nancylynnofficial.com
Email: nancylynnofficial@gmail.com

About the Author

Nancy is trained as a special education teacher and loves the beauty of classical music. She has spent most of her life searching for more of life's good things, and until recently, didn't realize she needed to think about and focus on the good as opposed to waiting for it to come. Her true desire is to transmit hope and healing to all people. She believes that there is a Higher Power filled with love, and that each of us has access to this love inside of us. We are powerful and magnificent beings who must own our power so we can live a life that we love.

With every donation, a voice will be given to the creativity that lies within the hearts of our children living with diverse challenges.

By making this difference, children that may not have been given the opportunity to have their Heart Heard will have the freedom to create beautiful works of art and musical creations.

Donate by visiting

HeartstobeHeard.com

We thank you.

www.ingramcontent.com/pod-product-compliance
Lightning Source LLC
Chambersburg PA
CBHW022108050726

47591CB00002B/712

Instructions for using AR

LET AUGMENTED REALITY CHANGE HOW YOU READ A BOOK

With your smartphone, iPad or tablet you can use the Neighbur Vue app to invoke the augmented reality experience to literally read outside the book.

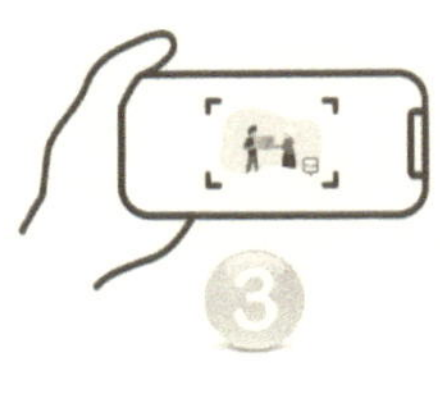

1. Notice the spelling: download the **Neighbur Vue** app from the Apple App Store or Google Play
2. Open and select the [vue] (vue) option
3. Point your lens at the full image with the [vue] and enjoy the augmented reality experience.

Go ahead and try it right now with the front cover of this book.

Once the content begins, click the **'Lock'** icon to lock the content onto your phone.